Shock & Roll

A Poppy Lewis Mystery

Book 5

Lucinda Harrison

Shock & Roll

ISBN: 978-1-7367596-4-6

To all the rock & rollers out there.

One

I UNFURLED THE small scrap of paper in my hands and spoke the message written within. "'Someone close to you will face an ominous threat.'" I glanced at the three women who assembled that evening in the quaint library at my bed-and-breakfast, the Pearl-by-the-Sea. Locking eyes with them one by one, I considered their fates.

"Oh no," my friend Angie Owens said. "That's terrible, Poppy. I hope it's not me." She glanced at the others with her brown doe eyes: Harper Tillman, long and lanky, and Greta, my elderly, unkempt cook and housekeeper. "But I don't want it to be any of you, either."

"My turn." Harper sat on the floor and leaned casually against the cushion of a leather club chair. Atop that cushion snored a fat ginger cat, oblivious to the goings on. Harper cleared her throat, uncurled her own strip of paper, then said, "'Lost in time, a secret will soon emerge.'" She tossed the paper onto the floor with the flick of a wrist. "Meh, sounds lame."

"That's not lame," Angie said. "Some secrets can be

exciting."

"Exciting in a bad way, in my experience," Harper said.

"What does yours say?" I asked Angie.

"'Givers of love will find happiness in life.'"

Harper snatched the scroll from Angie's pudgy hands and stared at the words. "Unbelievable. It's like it knows you."

"All right, Greta," I said, "you're the last one."

Greta tucked a greasy strand of gray hair behind a wrinkled ear and peered at the snippet of thin paper. She frowned and let out a grunt. "'Seven, forty-three, twenty-one, twenty-seven, nine, thirty.'"

"Those are your lucky numbers." I dropped my own fortune onto the coffee table and picked up my chopsticks to take another bite of noodles. "What does the other side say?"

"'Expect an upturn in your love life.'"

Harper snorted and choked as a noodle went down the wrong pipe. "Gah! Not likely."

"Harper," Angie admonished, "be nice. I think it would be lovely if Greta found a beau."

"One of my guests has a little crush on her," I said with a grin. "He keeps asking about her."

Greta recoiled and crumpled the fortune in her hand. "I'd rather have government probes shoved into my—"

"How about," I said, cutting her off, "we share our plans for the Mista Vista Pageant?"

"Absolute piffle," Greta mumbled.

I sighed. "A male pageant could be fun, and it supports the Vista County Animal Shelter, so don't complain. What about you, Angie? Is Roy up for it?"

She clapped her little hands in excitement. "He sure is. I can't wait to show him off. He has a good chance, too."

"Uh," Harper said, "he's got zero chance against my main man." She stroked the sleeping cat with her long fingers and he let out a slow stretch before curling up and going back to sleep.

"You aren't thinking of entering Mayor Dewey into the pageant?" Angie peered around, confused. "Can you enter a cat? Is that even allowed?"

Harper waved her off. "What I want to know is if Poppy's asked Ryan yet."

"Not yet," I admitted. "But I'm going to."

Harper twirled a dismissive finger in the air. "Promises, promises."

My friends, supportive after my divorce, were ready to see my romance with our resident pharmacist go to the next level. "There's still plenty of time to prepare. I'm asking him tomorrow."

Greta slumped deeper into the second leather club chair. "Can we get to the real reason we're here?"

I pulled out my phone and flipped through the photos until I came upon the one I needed. I set the phone in the middle of the coffee table and the four of us leaned in for a closer look. The photograph showed the disjointed back of an elaborate chair. Upholstery had been stripped away to reveal a set of markings on the wooden structure underneath. A sinuous line stretched from one side of the wood panel to the other, with a deliberate X inscribed at one end point. Other symbols tracked along the line's path, but they were unknown to us.

Angie sighed. "I still have no idea what it could be."

"Our minds need to marinate," Greta said.

"Hold on," Harper said, "aren't you supposed to be researching this map? Shouldn't you be out scouring manuscripts or something instead of freeloading off Poppy?"

"Ho ho," Greta said. "You weren't afraid to freeload yourself when you inhaled my pancakes this morning."

"Would you both cut it out?" I snapped. They quieted down, but their mutual glares remained.

Greta lowered her voice. "We should scan for listening devices before we say any more."

Angie gasped and clapped her hands over her mouth, as if she'd said something already.

"How would we even do that?" I asked. "Everett Ayers is long gone. And this isn't spy world, anyway. No one is listening in."

A knock on the library door made each of us jump. The door opened and a middle-aged man poked his head in. He wore his salt-and-pepper hair shoulder-length, and the deep lines of his face spoke of hard living. "I thought I heard you in here."

Greta harrumphed at this.

"You got any more towels?"

"Of course," I said. "There're more in the top cupboard in the bathroom."

He grunted in response, then closed the door behind him.

"He was awfully gruff," Angie said. "Is that one of the band members staying here?"

I nodded. "The lead singer, Tango McColl."

"Tango?" Harper asked with a scoff. "Is that his real name?"

"I think so," I said, "but he might be the only one—the rest all have crazy band nicknames like Hips and Wings. Even the band manager goes by the name Cabo, but his real name is Albert Goff according to the reservation."

"I think it's exciting," Angie said. "It's not every day that a rock band stays in little Starry Cove."

"Well," I said, "they've booked the Pearl for a few weeks, at least. They're working on a new album. This is some sort of creative retreat for them."

"Aging rock band trying to reinvigorate their careers." Harper almost laughed. "Isn't that a cliché? How old are these geezers, anyway?"

I shrugged. "No idea. Cabo said Tango's birthday is tomorrow, but I didn't ask how old he'd be. I'm guessing somewhere in his early sixties?"

"Probably younger," Harper said. "Rock music will age you exponentially."

"And how does that work with Lily staying here?" Angie asked. "Sounds like you have a full house."

Lily Lewis. My sister and current houseguest—not to be confused with my bed-and-breakfast guests—arrived somewhat unannounced a few weeks prior. "She's settling in."

"*Settling in*?" Harper repeated. "I thought she was only staying a few days. Now it's turned into weeks."

"Well," I said, picking at the tufting on a nearby throw pillow, "her condo remodel took an unexpected turn."

"But where's she been staying?" Angie asked. "All your rooms are full?"

At this, Greta harrumphed and crossed her arms, and

I shared her frustration. Our current living conditions weren't ideal. "She's staying in my room and I'm bunking with Greta."

Greta harrumphed again. "She won't let me clip my toenails in my own bed."

"Is Lily a paying guest?" Harper asked. "What could possess you to share a space with this one?" She shot a thumb Greta's way.

"Not exactly." I said with a sigh. "But she acts like one. There wasn't anywhere else to put her. I had the band coming and their stay was already paid for."

Harper eyed the older woman sideways. "You should have made Lily stay with Greta."

"Oh gosh," Angie said. "I'm sure that wouldn't have worked out."

"Yeah right," I said. "They're like two circling cats with their hackles raised. Besides, Lily's still in cancer treatments and she needs a tranquil space. Her hair's growing back, too. It's nearly down to her shoulders."

"That's so nice to hear," Angie said. "But the hair is the only way I can tell you two apart." She looked at me apologetically. "From a distance, at least. And she wears dresses. You don't wear dresses. Also, you're nicer when you talk to people, Poppy."

"Thanks."

"Are we almost done here?" Greta asked. "I'd like you all out of my library."

Harper shot a glare at Greta. "It's Poppy's library, you old scab."

I was too exhausted to get between them. "Let's wrap it up. I'm tired."

"Me too," Angie said, yawning. "Roy and I are up at

6

four o'clock tomorrow to open the bakery."

"I'll see you guys around then. The band is having their first practice at the community center. It's all set up, right Harper?"

"Huh? Oh, yeah. Everything's ready." She scooped Mayor Dewey into her arms without much fuss. "C'mon, little man, we've got a big day tomorrow."

***

The next morning, I heard the band warming up before I'd reached the community center down the road from the Pearl. A cacophony of notes, some from a guitar, some from the drums, and a dozen other jarring sounds flooded the small town's Main Street.

The double doors hung wide open and a small gathering of townspeople stared inside. Harper and Angie were among the group, and I sidled up beside them to watch the band.

"How exciting," Angie said, clapping her hands together. "What was the band's name again?"

"The Five Foxes," I said. "Apparently, they used to be a big deal. They had a number one hit a few decades ago called 'Drunk on the Nile.'"

A pained warble escaped from inside and the crowd flinched.

"What was that?" I asked. "Sounded like the final howl of a dying animal."

Harper stood on the tips of her toes. As the tallest member of our trio, she could see over the crowds. "I think... I think it's their singer, that Tango guy."

"What?" I asked, surprised. "He's so awful. I hope that's just his warm up."

7

Even Angie's enthusiasm waned. "That was pretty bad. Dewey made that sound once when Roy stepped on his tail. Did you say they had some number one hits once?"

I shrugged. "That's what they told me. Maybe he sounded better in his youth."

"Well," Harper said, peering around as the crowd dispersed. "At least that cleared off all the lookie-loos. I guess no one likes to listen to nails on a chalkboard."

We inched closer to the open doorway. Inside, I spotted Tango, who sat on one of the center's donated sofas canoodling with a sultry woman perched on his knee. Her smooth pale skin and lush red hair contrasted sharply against the older singer, and she trailed a long fake fingernail through his stringy salt-and-pepper hair.

"Is that a groupie?" Angie asked in a whisper.

"No," I said. "That's the lead singer's wife, Cherry."

"All right, Poppy," Harper said, "who the heck are all these people? They can't all be in the band."

I pointed toward a thin man with long, dirty blond hair at the far side of the room, furthest from Tango and Cherry. He wore a basic white T-shirt that fit too small and tight denim jeans with the knees ripped out. A thick leather belt with inset rhinestones sparkled at his waist. His attention was firmly on the tuning keys of his purple electric guitar. I allowed a small smile. The shade was close to the paint color of the Pearl. "That's Wings on lead guitar."

Harper gave him an approving once over. "He'd be kinda sexy if he wasn't the same age as my grandpa. And if I had any interest in men."

Tango let out another grating lyric and Cherry

giggled in his lap. Wings glared daggers across the room before returning to tuning his instrument.

"The one next to Wings is Dee. He's on drums."

"Drums are my favorite," Angie said before sheepishly adding, "Well, percussion, at least. I played the cymbals in high school."

Unlike the others, Dee appeared clean-cut with his short buzz and lack of facial hair. He'd told me that long hair was a nightmare when you were sweating onstage and thrashing your drumsticks around.

"Who's the giant?" Harper asked, nodding toward a towering man hiding behind a curtain of dark, wavy hair. He leaned against the wall in a faded green flannel and strummed idly at the strings of the bass guitar hanging at his left hip.

"That's Slomo."

"Slomo." Angie repeated the name like molasses. "How do you think he got that nickname?"

"Exactly the way you'd think. He talks slow. He moves slow."

"Does he think slow, too?" Harper quipped.

"He's not dumb," I said. "I think he's thoughtful and deliberate. But I never realized he was left-handed."

"Does that make a difference?" Angie asked.

"I don't think so. He just plays from the opposite hip. Speaking of hips..." I craned my neck to scan the room before settling on a slight man seated in the corner with a guitar perched on his lap. Strands of black hair were firmly tucked behind each ear, which only highlighted his recessing hairline. "That's Hips on rhythm guitar. He also does back-up vocals."

"If he's the back-up singer," Harper said in a low

voice, "I'd hate to hear what he sounds like after Tango."

As if on cue, Hips worked a kink from his knuckles, then strummed his guitar once and began to sing from the reverberating note. "*All is lost, can't be found. How's the weather when I come around?*"

My jaw dropped. Harper and Angie, too, couldn't find the words. Hips' voice was a blooming bouquet next to Tango's prickly weed. Smooth and silky, like butter.

Once she'd recovered, Harper turned to Angie and me. "Do you think he sounds that good because we're comparing him to that barking dog, Tango?"

"I don't think so," I said. "I got goosebumps."

Angie looked at her forearms. "Me too. Why is he the *back-up* singer?"

I shrugged. I wondered that too, but I knew this band had been together for over thirty years. "Maybe barking dog is the sound they're going for?"

From behind us came the disjointed jangle of a tambourine. We swiveled to see Greta sauntering up the walkway, banging the instrument wildly on her thigh. Her hair flowed loose and whipped in long strands as she flailed to the beat.

"Oh boy," said Harper. "Looks like Greta's gotten loose."

"Should Greta have percussion instruments?" Angie asked with a croak. "That seems like a bad idea."

As Greta gyrated her way to our side, I put out a hand to stop her. "What on earth are you doing? Did you take that from a guest's bag?"

"This?" Greta held up the tambourine and gave it a vigorous shake. My eyes flattened as the resonance died away and she added, "Of course not. It was a gift."

"From whom?" I demanded.

We followed Greta's gnarled finger toward the community center. A stout man of middle years with dribbles of sweat running down his face scurried about tending to seemingly important tasks. When he caught our stares, he stopped and smiled through a mouth of oafishly large teeth. He held up a hand, wiggling his fingers at Greta.

"That's Dutch," I said. "He's their roadie. Sets stuff up and runs errands, that sort of thing. He's also the one with a crush on Greta."

Angie nudged Greta in the side. "How sweet. He's got a thing for our girl."

"Unbelievable," Harper said through a phony dry heave.

"I thought you said you didn't want a beau?" Angie asked.

Greta scoffed. "I said I'd rather be probed by the government. I didn't say I wouldn't accept gifts." She rattled the tambourine in Angie's face and scampered away, jingling with every step.

"Good riddance," Harper said. "That thing's gonna get old real fast, Poppy."

"I know," I said with a sigh. "Why couldn't Dutch have given her flowers or chocolates like a normal crush?"

"Who's the last guy? He doesn't look like he fits with the others." Harper pointed at a bald man with leathery skin who spoke with animated gusto to Tango and Cherry. He wore sunglasses, even indoors, and a Hawaiian shirt covered in hula dancers wearing coconut bras and short grass skirts.

"That's the band manager, but he goes by the name

Cabo."

"As in Cabo San Lucas?" Harper asked.

I shrugged. "Their crazy nicknames must come from somewhere."

"Why can't people go by their given names?" Angie asked. "It's so much easier."

Harper scrunched up her face. "Even you go by a nickname, *Angela*."

Angie blushed and let out a faint giggle. "I suppose you're right."

"What in tarnation!" a voice called from across the street. Deputy Todd, the town's sole law enforcement officer, crossed the road in six long strides, his cowboy boots clopping with every step like a prancing show pony. The shade from the rim of his oversized sheriff's hat hid his face, but I knew he was angry.

"Hello, deputy," Harper said. "Out fighting the enemies of peace and justice, I see."

He shot Harper a look. "I'll get to you later." Then he turned his twitching mustache to me. "Miss Lewis, would you, for once, wrangle your unbridled housekeeper? She nearly took my head off swinging that razordrum around."

"Tambourine," I corrected.

"Don't get smart, Miss Lewis. Now I've also had a noise complaint about the hubbub going on here."

Harper crossed her arms. "Your wife's complaints don't count."

The deputy sputtered, "I'll have you—"

Harper cut in, "These fine gentlemen have paid a pretty penny to rent out our community center. Money this town could well use to patch the potholes, repaint the flower boxes, mow the grass on the roundabout—you get my meaning?"

"Well," he said, bristling, "these long-haired ruffi-ans—"

"Are guests at my bed-and-breakfast," I said, finishing the line for him.

Deputy Todd bristled, but in the meantime, the band had taken their spots, instruments in hand, and prepared to start their practice session.

"Here we go," Angie said, clutching her apron. Her smile spread from one chubby cheek to the other.

The decorative metal trinkets dangling from Tango's boots jangled as he slopped across the floor and stepped up to the microphone. He looked back at Cherry with a wink. She grinned back with a lascivious smile from the threadbare sofa. The other band members waited for their cue, eyes on Tango to begin their first song.

The lead singer closed his eyes and his lips parted with the first ragged note. "Aye—Ah!" Blue sparks flew and the spot where Tango stood lit up like a blazing fire-work. He flew backward, hitting his head on the corner of an amplifier and came to a landing atop a pile of empty instrument cases discarded toward the back of the room. Cherry's scream peeled through the air.

I blinked away the white afterimage that still seared my vision. "What was that?"

"I don't know," Harper said, "but I don't think it was supposed to happen."

We rushed through the doors, Deputy Todd in the lead, as the others crowded around Tango in a mass. "Get back," the deputy said with a growl. "I said get back." Nudging the slower movers out of the way, he kneeled beside Tango and placed two hands to his neck, checking for a pulse. The man's eyes were still closed and a faint black burn marred his lips.

He did not move.

The deputy placed his stiff-armed palms on the prostrate man's chest and began compressions.

"I'm calling 9-1-1," Angie told him and darted away from the scene.

"What's happening?" Cherry wailed. "What's happening?"

"You heard the man!" Cabo shouted. He held out an arm to keep Cherry at bay. "Stay back."

Harper waved a hand in front of her face. "What's that smell?"

"Smells like burnt hair," I said. "I think he's been electrocuted."

Two

HARPER, ANGIE, AND I stood back from the hubbub of medical personnel encircling Tango, who still lay on the floor. Cherry sobbed in great heaves into Dee's shoulder on the outskirts of the group. The drummer held her with one arm wrapped around her trembling shoulder. In the other he twirled a drumstick like a baton at his side, back and forth in swift motions like a nervous tick.

After an agonizingly long wait while CPR was administered, the medical technician finally stood up from the center of the circle. Everyone took a collective step back to give her room. She let out a deep sigh. "I'm so sorry. There's nothing else I can do."

A single wail rose from Cherry and she slumped into Dee's arms. He faltered under the weight, but caught her and carried her, half-stumbling, to the sofa along the wall.

I exchanged surprised looks with Harper and Angie, but did not interfere. We remained standing nearby.

Cabo ran both hands through his hair, turned away from the group, and seethed through pursed lips.

15

"Dead?" Slomo asked in a deep rumble, as though the word made no sense.

"This is crazy, man," Hips said with a hand at his temple. "Crazy."

Cabo swiveled back to the group. "I want everyone away from your instruments. Dutch," he called, zeroing in on the short balding man, "get these unplugged and packed up. This building is compromised."

Harper stepped forward. "Compromised? What's that supposed to mean?"

Cabo took three long strides toward Harper and whipped off his sunglasses. "My lead singer is *dead*," he spat. "I don't know what kind of haywire electrical system you have in this joint, but it's clearly unsafe."

"Unsafe?" Harper repeated with a scoff. "If this place can handle twenty thousand Christmas bulbs and the Starry Cove non-denominational festival tree *and* Mrs. Perez's creepy dancing holiday bear animatronics, it can definitely handle your measly band equipment."

"You saw those sparks." Cabo pointed toward the scene of Tango's electrocution. He took another step toward Harper and jabbed his finger her way. "I hope you have good insurance, because I'll be taking your little town to the cleaners for this."

The blood drained from Harper's face as Cabo turned and stomped away.

Angie peered up at Harper with her brown doe eyes. "He wouldn't think of suing the town, would he? Can he do that?"

"Ugh." Harper shook her fists at the overcast skies. "There's no way the community center wouldn't be able to handle their electrical equipment. Like I said, this place ran just fine lit up with the town's holiday setup, which was way more electrical mojo than what these guys brought."

"So," I said, "Tango's death was caused by something else."

"But he was clearly electrocuted." Angie swallowed hard and darted her eyes toward Tango's now-covered body. "We could smell him."

Harper gritted her teeth. "Now Deputy Todd's gonna want to shut down the community center and we've got the Mista Vista Pageant coming up."

"Gosh, someone died, Harper..."

"The timing is really bad, that's all I mean."

"Hold on," I said. "I'm still stuck on the idea that Tango's electrocution wasn't because of the building. What caused it then?"

The three of us exchanged concerned glances.

After a moment, Harper held up her hands in mock defense. "I'm not saying it would be good if this guy's death was because of something other than the community center but,"—she paused and caught my eye—"I kinda am."

I nodded. "If the town is in danger of a lawsuit, we need to find out what really happened to Tango."

***

The band coalesced back at the Pearl, but the mood was somber. They sat silently in the shared great room, lost in their own thoughts. I couldn't imagine what impact losing their leader would have, but this would definitely put a major kink in their comeback plans.

While my guests brooded, I wrangled Greta into

making tea while I prepared a fresh plate of cheese and crackers. Perhaps some snacks would break the heavy silence.

Greta poked her head through the swivel door from the kitchen, which looked out onto the main living area through the dining room. "What did you do to them? They look like a gang of zombies."

"I didn't do anything to them. I told you their singer had an accident and died."

She sniffed and ducked her head back into the kitchen. "It's going to take more than cheese to get them out of their funk. Maybe I should add a few of my special treats to the platter…"

"No," I said sharply. "No special treats. I can't afford another mishap. You take the cheese and I'll grab the tea."

"What you call a mishap, I call a success, but suit yourself." Greta wiped her hands in two great strokes on her apron and lifted the cheese platter high onto one shoulder. At her stunted height, Greta's shoulder was barely chest high on me, and I reached over to fix a misarranged cheddar cube before waving her through the swivel door.

"It's not your fault, Dutch," Cabo said as we entered. "You've never had an accident before. It was clearly this negligent town's electrical system."

Dutch's face pressed deep into his hands, and jerky heaves accompanied his tears. He'd appeared inconsolable since Tango's death. I'd hoped a nibble of cheese would raise the band's spirits, but now, seeing their faces, it felt like a weak and tactless gesture in the face of their grief.

It also hurt personally to hear my town called negligent. Harper certainly would never be lax with potential liabilities. Although I remembered the gigantic pothole on Main Street that still hadn't been addressed, and those tree branches that hung low over the first Stop sign into town sure were a hazard. I shook those out of my head, though. I had seen the holiday light displays myself, and if the community center could survive that excessive surge of twinkling, animatronic power, it could survive anything.

Greta and I slipped the tea and cheese plate onto the banquette in the dining space and announced that the group could help themselves at their leisure. A few mumbled words of thanks floated our way, but no one stirred.

"What are we gonna do now?" Hips asked Cabo.

"Yeah," Slomo said, "what now?"

Wings folded his arms defiantly. "I'm not going back in that building."

"We can't continue," Dee said. "Tango's gone, and we should all leave, too."

"All right, all right." Cabo held up his hands to shush the chatter. "Just let me think."

"And what about Cherry?" Dee asked.

Everyone turned to Cherry, who huddled with her knees close to her chest in the large velvet fireside chair. Rivulets of wet and dried mascara tarnished her cheeks and her eyes, half-lidded, were bloodshot from crying.

"She's just lost her husband and we're all sitting around here like a bunch of bums."

"You want to just go home?" Cabo asked with a twinge of scandalized surprise in his voice. "Go home?" He spread his hands wide. "We've paid for all of this.

This is supposed to be our comeback, remember? Hunker down and spit out an album, back to the top of the charts, world tour, the whole shebang. We can't let that go now."

"You expect us to stay?" Hips asked, incredulous.

"Why not?" Cabo said. "It's what Tango would have wanted. He was one-hundred percent on board with this plan. He was ready, willing." Cabo clenched his fists and turned to face each band member. "He was hungry for it."

Slomo shook his head. "I don't know, man."

Wings spread his arms out dramatically. "If you haven't noticed, we don't have a lead singer."

"We've got Hips." Dutch nodded toward the backup singer. "He knows all the songs."

"Now hold on," Hips said. "I can't take the place of Tango. He's our front man. Wouldn't it be disrespectful to him to—"

Cabo cut him off. "We make it a tribute album." He turned to Cherry. "How does that sound? A tribute to Tango."

Dee eyed Cherry with concern.

"A tribute," Cherry repeated through trembling lips, mulling over the words before nodding. "Tango would have liked that."

"Excellent," Cabo said, rubbing his hands together. "Dutch, you're now on rhythm guitar and backup vocals."

"Me?" Dutch stammered, eyes wide.

Slomo swung his half-lidded eyes toward Cabo and opened his mouth to say something, but was cut off by the manager.

"Now," Cabo said, "we just need a new location to set up." He turned my way and raised an eyebrow.

"Uh." I'd been so engrossed in listening to my guests

that I forgot they could see Greta and I were still there. "The community center's the most obvious place. If you don't want to play there, I'm not sure what options there are."

Hips said, "We'll need a location that has enough room for all of us and our stuff."

"And not too far from here," Cabo said. "I don't want to pay for extra transportation."

"Good acoustics," Slomo added.

"Huh." Greta sniffed and adjusted her skirt with a heft. "Sounds just like the basement, doesn't it, Poppy?"

In an instant, my stomach dropped, and I let out a low, strangled gurgle.

Three

"I DON'T KNOW why you're mad," Greta said the next morning as we prepared breakfast. "I was trying to be helpful."

"I'm not mad," I said through gritted teeth. "I just wish you would hold your tongue sometimes."

Greta knocked a small wooden stool with her tiny foot and it skidded across the floor, landing in front of the sink. The tambourine dangling from her belt jingled as she hopped onto the step and began to rinse a large stainless steel pot. "Suit yourself," she said, "but I remember you telling me to be more helpful to the guests."

I stopped wiping down the plate I held in my left hand and sighed. "I meant I wanted you to respond to their questions rather than huff at them and skitter away like a frightened bunny."

Greta huffed. "And did I do that? No. I answered their question. I was *helpful*."

"And now I have an entire band setting up shop in my basement, thanks to you. The entire house will be filled with rock music dawn 'til dusk."

"Sounds like a hoot to me." Greta wiggled her butt from atop the stool. Her long, gray housedress swayed along with her.

"I still haven't covered up the entry to Arthur's secret room down there. It looks like I have an underground dungeon or something."

"Hmm," Greta mumbled. "Arthur." She pursed her lips as she hauled the pot from the sink. "I still don't understand why he didn't tell me he was Claude Goodwin's heir."

I bit my lip, not wanting to upset her. "Maybe he was trying to protect you? If he knew the Gold Hand—and Everett Goodwin—were after what he had, keeping you in the dark may have been the safest thing."

"Harrumph." Greta trudged to the table where we'd set out the morning's breakfast trays. "Let's get this service out. I need to meet Moira at the library later."

"You and Moira have become close."

She eyed me sideways as she swiveled through the door from the kitchen to the dining room. "Yeah? So what? You said I needed friends."

I chuckled in response. "So I did."

As we entered the dining room, the noise from the chattering guests drowned us out. My eyes narrowed as I spotted Lily seated at one end of the long table, dining as a guest instead of helping Greta and me in the kitchen. That irritation slid off me as I scanned to Cherry, still sad and solemn seated next to Dee, who whispered softly to her.

Greta and I placed the serving trays on the buffet along the wall and prepared to serve breakfast. Today was

Greta's hash, and it hit all the marks: steak, potatoes, peppers, sweet onion, and a sunny-side up egg for each plate. A light drizzle of a spicy homemade ketchup—which she swore contained no illicit drugs this time—finished it off.

Dutch had his fork in hand, eager to dive in. "That looks mighty tasty, Greta."

Greta mumbled a response as she served around the table, scooping out a generous portion to each guest and I followed behind to top with the egg. A basket of toast and a selection of morning beverages completed the table.

Cabo and Dutch wasted no time hefting mouthfuls of steak and egg into their mouths, while others, like Hips, Dee, and Cherry, pushed the hash around with their forks, not eating much. Lily's short black hair fell over her face, but failed to hide the hint of revulsion as she segregated the fried potatoes to one side of her plate.

I was about to take my place at the table when the doorbell rang. Excusing myself, I followed the path from the dining room and into the foyer. At the sidelights next to the ornate door, I could make out the indistinct shape of a person with their face pressed up against the glass, trying to see through. There was one thing I could make out, though: red glasses. I cringed, and for a moment I debated simply returning to my meal and hoping the figure would go away, but the next ring of the doorbell told me I was out of luck. Sighing, I opened the door.

"Poppy Lewis," Veronica Valentine said my name with the hint of a sneer, as though I'd done something naughty. Her blonde bob was cut sharp enough to slash through steel, and she already held up a recording device to capture our conversation.

I crossed my arms. "What do you want, Veronica?"

"I just want to talk, of course. The *Vista View* is always looking for the next big story." She tried to peer past me into the house, but I sidestepped to block her view. "What are you hiding in there, Poppy?"

"None of your business," I said. "Speaking of which, what exactly is your business? I'm busy."

"I came to town to do a story on the Mista Vista Pageant, but now I hear there's been a death and, well," she cocked her head, "death trumps pageant."

I shook my head in disgust. "It's not a game of rock, paper, scissors, Veronica. And I'm not sharing any information with you."

"Fine," she said with a blaze of disappointment in her eyes. "Then what about the Mista Vista Pageant? I'll be on the judging panel since the paper is sponsoring the event, after all." She eyed me slyly. "I don't suppose you have an entrant? Maybe that will loosen your lips a little to—"

I slammed the door in Veronica's face. Sneaky snake of a woman. My body shook with rage and I leaned against the door, letting it wash over me. A small mirror hung from the wall by the door and I took a quick glance, patting my cheeks and waited for the red blotches on my skin to fade.

The doorbell rung again, and I felt the heat rising once more. That woman didn't know when to quit. I swung the door open. "Get lost," I seethed before choking on the last word. Deputy Todd, in full uniform, glared at me from under the brim of his sheriff's hat.

"Excuse me?" he asked in a long drawl.

"Uh, sorry, deputy," I said, eyes flicking toward the street in search of Veronica. "I thought you were someone else."

"Mm-hmm," he mumbled beneath his mustache, seemingly unconvinced. "I need a word, Miss Lewis."

"Of course," I said and stepped onto the porch, closing the door behind me.

"I wanted to catch you and your guests before anyone leaves. The whole community center's been shut down for a full electrical inspection. The results are going to take a while, but in the meantime, I'm going to need the contact information for your guests before they leave town today."

"Shut down?"

He nodded. "Safety protocols. Now, I'll need to speak with your guests. Get their information, that sort of thing."

"They're not leaving town."

"They aren't?" His hat wobbled in surprise.

"No, they've decided to carry on with their album." I forced a smile. "Using my basement."

He puffed out his mustache. "In that case," he said sternly, "I hope there won't be any noise complaints."

"Are broken noise ordinances really the most pressing matter for law enforcement right now?"

Deputy Todd pointed a finger at me. "Just stay within the law, Miss Lewis, and we won't have any problem. And don't even think about getting involved in my investigation. Got it?"

My jaw clenched. "Got it."

***

Greta had begged to leave after breakfast. She was eager to get to the library, and I complied, not wanting to impede her budding friendship with Moira, a librarian at the Vista County Library. I'd even agreed to turn down the rooms by myself so she could take the scooter and enjoy the rest of her morning. My agreeable mood surprised me, considering I'd had not one, but two unwanted visitors and that usually put me on edge. Maybe Greta *did* put something in that sauce.

Either way, I bounded down the sidewalk to Angie's nearby bakery once the chores were done.

"Hi Poppy," Angie said cheerfully as I stepped into the bakery, the bell above the door giving me away.

"Hey there." I smiled at Shelby, the owner of the diner, who stood across the counter from Angie. Her signature beehive and accompanying barrettes towered over my diminutive friend. She must have popped over from next door, since she still wore her diner uniform and apron.

"Hi there, dearie." Shelby acknowledged me with a wave before turning back to Angie. "Like I was saying, we should go with the choux pastry cheese puffs. Those were a big hit last time."

"I don't know," Angie said, biting her lip. "I really wanted to incorporate Bruno Hauser's sourdough. Maybe in a crostini?"

"You can do your great-whatever-grandpa's sourdough, too. But those cheese puffs..." Shelby smacked her lips. "Devine, dearie."

I spotted Harper slumped in a chair at the lone table, droopy-eyed from boredom, no doubt. She wore her mail carrier's uniform along with a brightly colored rainbow headband to hold back a riot of dark brown curls.

"Sit," she said, motioning me to the other chair with

a lazy flap of her wrist. "These two have been clucking about their catering business all morning."

"Sounds like it's really taking off."

"Yeah," Harper said. "I think they have a few events in the pipeline."

Angie wandered over with a coffee mug in one hand and a steaming hot cinnamon roll in the other. She set them in front of me and placed a hand on my shoulder. "How are you and your guests doing after yesterday?"

The sincerity in her voice was touching. Angie always mothered Harper and me, even though she was only a few years older than I was. "I'm fine. They're... okay, considering."

Angie nodded, and her sweet brown eyes comforted me.

"And thanks to Greta," I said, "they'll be practicing for the new album in my basement."

These last words jolted Harper from her daze. "The basement?" Her eyes shifted from me to Angie, then to Shelby, who waited at the counter for Angie to return. Her voice lowered, and she asked, "What about, uh, your uncle's secret room?"

I shrugged. "It's empty."

"And creepy," Harper added.

"I keep telling you it would make a wonderful root cellar," Angie said. "Or a wine cellar."

I waved them off. "I know. And I have plans for that, but I haven't gotten to them yet. For now, it will just have to look like a dungeon. They're a rock band—maybe they'll think it's cool."

"Maybe you should move Greta down there?" Harper gave me the side eye and grinned.

"What about Cabo?" Angie asked. "Is he still thinking of suing the town?"

Harper groaned before slumping further in her chair.

"I don't know," I said. "Seems like it, though. I'm trying to be as accommodating as possible for now. Deputy Todd stopped by, too."

Angie's eyes widened. "What did he want?"

"Said they're investigating the electrical system at the community center and wanted to make sure my guests didn't leave. But since they're doing this tribute album now, they're staying for at least the remainder of their reservation at the Pearl."

"Investigating the electrical system," Harper repeated with a sneer. "With our luck, they'll hire our old friend Cho to do the work."

At the mention of Cho's name, Angie shivered, and I shot Harper a look of warning. Cho, my onetime electrician, turned out to be in cahoots with Dr. Goodwin, and we were careful not to speak too openly of Gold Hand operatives.

"What?" Harper said defensively. "It was just a joke."

"Joke or not," I said, "we should stay on our toes. We've seen no hint of the Gold Hand since Everett Goodwin left his threatening calling card at the Pearl. They could be lurking anywhere."

Angie nodded and swiveled her head around the bakery as if they may be hiding behind the pastry case.

Shelby sauntered to our side of the bakery. She clapped her hands with a smack and rubbed them together. "Which of you ladies is entering the Mista Vista Pageant? I've been grooming Nick Christos for weeks, dearies, and I don't see how anyone could beat Vista County's only Greek god."

I pursed my lips. Of course Shelby would snag Nick. Nick Christos, unfathomably, gobsmackingly handsome Nick Christos. Youthful, chiseled features, with shiny blond locks set off by his effortless tan. In the Pacific Northwest, tans were scarce unless through a bottle or a tanning bed. He was so gorgeous that there was a trick known to the ladies of Starry Cove to look just over Nick's shoulder when speaking with him, lest you fall into a blubbering puddle of goo while staring into his soft blue eyes.

"Poppy had better ask Ryan soon," Harper said. "If she's going to at all, that is."

"I am," I said quickly. "Today."

Harper shrugged and rolled her eyes with a dramatic lift of her eyebrows.

"What about you, dearie?" Shelby asked Angie.

"Roy already said he would do it. I wasn't sure at first, but he surprised me."

"Well," Shelby said with a twinkle in her eye, "you know the trophy isn't for the men, dearies—it's for the women who enter them."

"Nick may be hard to beat," Harper said, "but not impossible. I think Mayor Dewey could give him a run for his money."

Shelby's hands went to her hips and her beehive wobbled a few seconds before coming to rest. "You're entering the mayor? Isn't that a conflict of interest?"

Harper waved her off. "The contract for this thing was signed way before Dewey was elected. Besides, he's got to represent the town. He's practically *obligated* to enter."

Shelby's brow told me she wasn't so sure, and Angie just clicked her tongue, probably not wanting to revisit the matter.

Harper popped out of her seat and grabbed the mail-bag slung across the chair back. "Gotta go. Last stop is Treasures of the Coast way out on the Coastal Road."

Angie, Shelby, and I watched as Harper passed the front window, a smile spread ear-to-ear as her brown curls bounced along with each step.

"She's awfully excited about delivering mail today," Angie said.

A slight grin touched my lips. "Delivering to the Treasures of the Coast, at least."

***

I left the bakery and checked both ways on Main Street before crossing. The town pharmacy was tucked away in a little alcove in the back of the general store across from the diner and bakery. The time had come to face my fear and ask Ryan to enter the Mista Vista Pageant.

As I stepped onto the curb in front of the pharmacy, I spied Cherry's fiery red hair from a distance. She and Dee were making their way up the sidewalk where I'd just been. They must be out for lunch before the band began their practice session this afternoon. Cherry leaned against Dee's shoulder as they walked, and it occurred to me they seemed a bit too intimate for a woman who'd just lost her husband and a man who'd just lost his friend. He held her hand cradled in his arm and patted it warmly as they drifted toward the diner and disappeared inside.

Pushing the glass door open, I entered the general

store and waved hello to Ursula, the owner, who stood at the end of an aisle checking things off on a clipboard.

"Hi Poppy. You here to see Ryan?"

"Yeah."

She motioned to the pharmacy cubby with a quick flip of her head. "In the back."

"Thanks," I said. It took a few steps before I noticed Ethan, Ryan's son, standing behind the counter glowering at a haphazard mound of individually wrapped snacks piled high on the countertop. "Hi Ethan," I said with a friendly wave.

His head rose, and he raised a single hand in acknowledgement, then returned his focus to the pile.

Ryan wore a lovely periwinkle V-neck sweater beneath his customary white lab coat. Unassuming, but handsome in a cozy non-threatening way, his brown hair fell in just the right way, and his blue eyes sparkled behind delicate glasses. Just the sight of him gave me butterflies. Although it had been stewing for a while, we'd only recently made our coupledom official.

"Hello there," he said, spotting me. His thick Scottish accent always made me smile.

"I see Ursula's put Ethan to work."

"Aye," Ryan said, "put him to work and not ten minutes in he knocks over the beef jerky stand. Now he's got to sort all the flavors out—Barbeque, Sweet and Spicy, Teriyaki, and something called Fire Engine. I'd stay away from that one, if I were you."

"That would explain his sour face."

Ryan chuckled. "He's got to put in a hundred hours of volunteer work this term for school. Between you and me, I'm hoping it builds some character."

I nodded, knowingly. Ryan's turbulent relationship with his son was nothing new. Ethan was a young teen who'd lost his mother and acted out. "How's his wood-working going?"

"Also good. Thanks again for the suggestion. He's built approximately a thousand birdhouses and is probably ready to rebuild the backyard gazebo."

"Don't thank me yet," I said. "I have something to ask and you might not like it."

His eyebrow rose. "Oh? That's intriguing and frightening at the same time."

"Depends on how you look at it." I gave him my broadest, most sincere smile and batted my eyelashes to excess. "I wanted to ask if you would enter the Mista Vista Pageant." I left my wide eyes gazing into his, hoping to mesmerize him into agreement.

His response was as lukewarm as I'd expected. "Eh, that man pageant thing?" he asked. "I don't know, Poppy." He gave himself a once over. "That seems a bit out of my wheelhouse, don't you think?"

"Nonsense," I said. "You're an absolute hunk. And it's for a good cause. All proceeds benefit the Vista County Animal Shelter. You wouldn't want to disappoint all those puppies, would you?" My eyelashes fluttered again.

He groaned. "Ethan will rip me to shreds. I'll never live it down. Any credibility I've built as a cool dad will be completely demolished."

"Don't worry about Ethan," I said. "All teenagers are embarrassed of their parents. And you might have fun."

Ryan pushed his glasses up on his nose and eyed me askance. "What's in it for me?"

"Besides saving puppies?"

"Besides saving puppies," he said. "How about a date?"

"That's it?" I said, lighting up. "You'll do it in exchange for a date?"

He sighed, then smiled and let out a light chuckle. "I suppose if it will make you happy."

I clapped my hands together in excitement. "It will be a lot of fun, I promise."

"If you say so," he said skeptically, "but there'd better not be a swimsuit competition. This dad bod is not ready for prime time."

"Nothing like that," I said. "Just cultural style, talent, a brief interview, and something they're calling the Men and Mutts Parade."

Ryan gaped. "Parade? I'm not—"

The door chimed open, catching our attention, and Hips' slight frame stepped through the doorway. When he spotted the pharmacy counter, he made his way over.

"Hey." Hips nodded my direction.

"Hello there." I stepped away from the counter, giving Hips and the pharmacist little distance, and pretended to riffle through a rack of informational pamphlets on diabetes.

Hips stepped up to the counter. "I was hoping you could help me with some pain I've been having."

"Where's the pain located?" Ryan asked.

Hips rubbed at his right hand. "Here, in the fingers."

Ryan nodded knowingly. "You're a guitarist, aye?"

"Yeah, how'd you know?"

Ryan bobbed his head my way.

They both caught me watching, so I quickly averted

my eyes, engrossed now in a flyer on the benefits of a Mediterranean Diet.

Ryan continued, "Pain in your fingers could be signs of inflammation." He grabbed a bottle from a display stand. The pills inside rattled as he handed it to Hips. "These might help. Take one every four hours with a glass of water."

I thought to myself how aging must be awful, but soon remembered I'd already felt the effects of it myself while gardening. Achy back, stiff joints. Hips was at least another generation older than me, and he'd lived a hard rock life. Strumming those guitar strings all day must really take a toll. I caught myself, though, and remembered that Hips was now the singer and Dutch had taken over on rhythm guitar. What a break for Hips.

Wait a second.

My eyes narrowed, and I stole a glance at the older man, his black hair tucked neatly behind his ear. Out of all the band members, Hips seemed to have come out with the best outcome of all—newly anointed lead singer and no more pesky guitar to inflame his achy joints.

"Anything else?" Ryan asked.

"Uh, yeah," Hips said. "Do you have any strong sleeping pills?"

Sleeping Pills? Now my interest was really piqued.

"I'm afraid you'll need a prescription for those."

Hips bit his lower lip.

"How about some melatonin?" Ryan pulled down another bottle, smaller than the first, and handed it to Hips. "Over-the-counter stuff. It won't knock you out, but it should help a bit and it won't interfere with those." He pointed to the other bottle in Hips' hand.

35

"Thanks," Hips said. "I'm a pretty light sleeper and my roommate snores."

Facing away from the two, I cringed and had to agree with Hips. Wings, his roommate, could use a nasal strip or two.

Hips thanked Ryan and left the shop with a small wave. I followed the singer with my eyes, wondering what a boon Tango's death had been for him. Once he was out of sight, I returned to Ryan's side.

"Now," he said, "what's this about a parade?"

"It's nothing, just a few dogs on leashes to wow the crowd. You like dogs, right? You'll love it."

"Mm-hmm."

He didn't sound convinced, but I took his silent displeasure as a sign of acquiescence.

"Good. Now that that's settled. We'll need to find a time to practice."

"Practice?" Ryan's voiced cracked in defeat.

Four

WITH RYAN ON board for the pageant, I felt good stepping through the doorway to the Pearl, but my smile quickly faded. Lily, dressed in a designer frock of classic silhouette that highlighted her figure, stood near the wooden credenza in the foyer. She held my hammered brass umbrella stand in her hands.

"What are you doing?" I asked. "Put that down."

Lily gave me an exasperated look, and let out a small laugh of derision. "You told me to make myself useful. Well, this thing," she held up the umbrella stand, "is hideous, so I'm removing it."

"That *thing* is an antique. And I paid good money for it."

Lily twisted her lip and glanced at the stand, then sighed. "I can't fix your bad taste, Poppy." She set the stand back on the floor between the end of the credenza and the carved newel post of the staircase. "Don't say I never tried to help."

"I meant something more like sweeping or dusting.

Maybe wash a dish or two."

"Isn't that why you have a housekeeper?"

I poked my head into the kitchen through the door from the foyer. "Where is Greta, anyway?"

"Don't ask me," Lily said, affronted. "I certainly don't keep tabs on her."

"Greta?" A voice called from the large living space. Dutch appeared a moment later, two guitars clasped by the neck in either hand. "I heard she was heading to the library. Not this one." He motioned to the remaining door off the foyer, which led to my small personal library. "The big one in Vista. I think that's what she said, anyway." His cheeks flushed. "She took my tambourine with her."

"Thanks, Dutch," I said.

Lily simply folded her arms and looked bored.

"Let me help you with those." I grabbed one of the guitars and motioned for Dutch to lead the way. Before we disappeared through the door from the foyer, I spared one last exasperated look at Lily, who ignored me.

I followed Dutch down the steps from the kitchen to my sizable basement. The sprawling space was large enough to serve as my long-term storage and still allow for the band to spread out with room to spare. During renovations the previous year, I'd installed additional lighting, which replaced the single bare bulb that used to illuminate the basement. Now, instead of creepy horror-movie lighting, the windowless space was lit up like a department store.

As soon as I'd stepped off the last stair, Hips' vocal warmups resonated through the basement. I shook my head, wondering how the band ever thought Tango was a better vocal choice than Hips.

"... not going to practice in that death trap—" Cabo's words cut off as he saw me. He reddened only a little before he stiffened his lip, his face taking on a look of defiance mixed with righteousness.

Dutch took the guitar from me and placed it with others set up against one wall. They were all there, the band, the manager, and the widow, in various stages of preparation. Dee secured cymbals to his drum set in one corner while Wings leaned against a wall, tightening a peg on the head of his guitar.

"Cool space," Slomo said in his lazy way, nodding toward me through his curtain of hair.

"What's with the weird little room off the back?" Dee tilted his head toward an outcropping in the rectangular basement.

I gritted my teeth. The room stood out like a sore thumb, jutting into the space underneath the living room. The walls were rough, not like the smooth concrete of the rest of the basement, and the color was off—a darker gray, making the alcove appear even smaller. Clearly, it had been added at a later date. "Future wine cellar," I said, hoping that would be the end of it.

"Looks like a torture chamber," Wings said. "Would be cool for an album cover."

"It's not a torture chamber," I assured them.

A grin spread across Wings' face. "You hidin' bodies down here, Poppy?"

That caused a laugh from all of them, and I chuckled nervously. "Only those who don't pay their reservation fee," I said. This brought on even more laughter, except from Cabo, who frowned and grumbled under his breath.

The truth was, that little room had once hidden a very large secret. It was the previous tomb of a small tome, hidden years earlier by my late uncle, Arthur, and held secrets to a long-ago treasure. I'd locked that notebook away in a safer place, but the scar in my basement remained.

Cabo clapped his hands together for attention. "All right, everyone, let's focus. We've lost time already, so I think we should dive right in to the song choices. With this new tribute bent, we may be limited."

"Don't worry about it," Wings said. "I've got plenty of new songs."

"I know Tango had written some new material." Dee rustled through a bag beside his chair.

I squinted and realized it was one of my yellow kitchen table chairs. Looking around, it seemed they'd pilfered all four of the chairs from the small breakfast table in one corner of my kitchen.

"Here they are," Dee said, holding up a few sheets of loose paper.

Wings grabbed them out of his hand and gave them a once over. He let out a huff of derision and shook the papers "Just what I thought—he didn't write these." Wings tossed the papers back at the drummer and they flew wildly, catching the air. "Tango couldn't write an original lyric to save his life."

Dee snatched the flying papers out of the air. "That's cold, man. He's dead." Dee's eyes spared a moment for Cherry, who swallowed repeatedly, her eyes welling with tears.

"Just shut up for once, would you Wings?" Cherry shouted, then brushed past me and stormed up the basement steps. Dee rushed after her, taking the steps two at a time.

"Nice job," Hips said to Wings. "You couldn't leave well enough alone?" Then he joined Dee and Cherry upstairs, exposing his loyalty.

"Dude…" Slomo said to Wings, shaking his head. He set his guitar gently on his chair and followed Hips upstairs.

Cabo threw up his arms. "Great," he said. "I've lost the entire band." He made his way toward the staircase. "I need a drink or something. Dutch?" Cabo waited for Dutch to scuttle up behind him. "No telling how long this meltdown might take. Probably a good time to bring out the remaining amps." Dutch nodded, and they both disappeared into the house above.

Wings remained leaned up against one basement wall. His jaw clenched, and he paid a little too much attention to the same tuning key, twisting it tighter and tighter.

"What was that all about?" I asked.

"Nothing," Wings said, but I could tell it ate at him. A moment later he said, "It's just that they all seem to think Tango was some great creative mind, you know?"

"He wasn't?"

Wings stopped tuning his guitar. "Remember the lyrics to 'One Hand on the Bottle'?"

I frowned. "Not really," I admitted.

Wings shook his head. "Doesn't matter. But I wrote those, not Tango, and it was one of our biggest hits. None of these guys," he motioned up the staircase, "seem to remember that." He took a few deep breaths and let the frustration subside. "I'm sad to lose Tango, okay, but we don't need him."

"That sounds a bit harsh."

"Harsh?" Wings repeated. "Did you hear his voice? That was harsh. And it brought us down. Now, that ain't my fault. It was Tango's fault."

I said nothing and just twisted my lip, feeling awkward and sad at the whole situation.

Wings shook his head again and went back to tuning. "There's just a lot of history in this band, and not all of it good."

"Like what?" I asked, stepping closer to Wings. "Anything bad enough that someone would want to hurt Tango?"

Wings' head shot up, his eyes wide, clearly surprised by my question. But a noise at the stairs caught our attention, and we watched as Cabo, followed by Hips, Slomo, and Dutch, descended the stairs. Dee and Cherry returned a few steps behind the others.

Before the group got close enough to hear, Wings whispered, "Let's just say there are a lot of intertwining relationships."

***

The band finally shuffled upstairs later that evening after a string on Slomo's bass broke for the second time. Greta and I were in the kitchen, me preparing evening snacks, and Greta still wiggling to the leftover tunes strumming through her head while banging on her tambourine.

"All done?" I called out hopefully, sparing a glare at Greta as Cabo and the others slogged through the kitchen and into the main seating area.

"For tonight," Cabo said. He stayed behind and let

the others file past, Greta on their heels, then he turned to me. "I need your help."

"My help?" I asked, surprised.

"I need a venue," he said in a low, hushed tone. His eyes flicked toward the door through which the band had retreated. "We need a gig. But not just any gig—I want something small, nothing big, nothing splashy. Something, you know, cozy."

"Cozy," I repeated, nodding along.

"Some place where we can be anonymous, try out our new stuff without the media's gaze, that sort of thing."

I gave him a flat stare. "Like the community center?"

He hissed. "Not that death trap."

I shot back, "It's not a death trap."

"Look," he said, sparing another glance toward the living room, "can you help or not? These guys need to see some action. They're like wilted noodles."

"Their friend just died, what do you expect?"

Cabo grimaced. "I know, I know. But we need a show. So, any ideas?"

His request made me grumble. Although Cabo and the band were paying guests, Cabo had still threatened to sue my little town, so my kindness could only go so far. "Maybe the reservation casino."

Cabo waved his hands immediately. "Too public. Too many cameras. Definitely not. We need something small. Something out of the way. A real hole in the wall."

"Well," I said, "if it's a hole in the wall you want, I know just the place. We can check it out tomorrow afternoon."

Cabo's eyes brightened. "Excellent." Then Cabo

leaned in. "Can you keep this between us? At least for now? I don't want the press getting wind of it and lurk about after what happened to Tango." His eyes narrowed. "And I need to keep an eye on Cherry, keep her from contacting the media."

"Why?"

Cabo rolled his eyes dramatically. "Drama queen. She's in it for the publicity. It's such a hassle having to work with her."

"I thought she was just here for Tango?"

"She was, but now that he's gone, she's got part ownership of the band." He scoffed, then mumbled under his breath, "Wants to stick her blubbering nose into everything."

"Wait," I said, "will Cherry inherit everything from Tango?"

Cabo raised both eyebrows at me as if I'd missed something obvious. "Oh, I'm sure of it. The band, the money, all of it." He leaned back against the counter and crossed his arms. "Right now, that widow's sitting mighty pretty."

Five

THE FOLLOWING MORNING, Lily managed to drag herself out of bed and 'help' with the morning breakfast preparation. This consisted of sitting at the kitchen table—after I hauled a chair up from the basement—and reading the morning's newspaper while Greta and I did all the work. At least it was a beautiful, sunny day. The fog had burned off early, leaving us with blue skies and only a few puffy white clouds I could make out through the kitchen windows.

Greta, perched on her wooden stool in front of the hot stove, hummed a tune I recognized from the band's practice the previous day. Her hips swayed, and the tambourine jingled faintly at her side.

"You were at the library pretty late last night," I said to her.

Her hips stopped gyrating. "Been helping Moira."

I nodded sagely, hinting that I was sure there was more to the story, but she only grunted and continued stirring. "I hope you're not losing interest in our own little mystery?" I kept my voice low, even though I was sure Lily was too absorbed in her own reading to listen in.

Greta tapped her spoon with extra force on the side of the pot. "There's not much to go on except a few scribbles on the back of a chair. I can't produce miracles, you know."

"Listen here," Lily said, clearing her throat and giving the paper a flick to straighten out the pages. "That reporter woman's written an article about the dead musician."

I stepped to the table in one long stride and snatched the paper from Lily's hands. My eyes scanned the headline before I read it aloud.

Aged Rocker Death Shocker

The sudden and tragic death of rocker Tango McColl has rocked the music world, leaving former hit-makers The Five Foxes in tatters. An insider source tells the *Vista View* that McColl's last moments were spent at the run-down community center in the tiny Vista County town of Starry Cove. That same source shared that McColl was horrifically electrocuted during the band's first rehearsal, which shocked not only McColl, but the band's adoring spectators, and left an acrid stench wafting on the salty sea air.

No official statement has been released by authorities, but our source indicated faulty electrical wiring may be to blame.

The *Vista View* reached out to Starry Cove's mayor for comment, but our calls were not returned by the time of publication.

I crumpled the paper in my hands and seethed. "Of course he didn't return their calls. He's a cat, for Pete's sake!"

"Sounds like your little town is in big trouble," Lily said before taking a sip of her tea.

"Cabo warned me about this," I said. "I'll bet that *insider source* is Cherry McColl, churning up publicity."

The back door to the kitchen, which led onto the wrap-around porch, swung open, hitting the wall and bouncing back as Harper hurried through, mail bag swinging wildly. "Is Dewey here?" Her head swung around, searching every corner of the room.

"No," I said. "What's wrong?"

She ducked and peered under the table before straightening up. "He's missing."

My fingers worked behind my back, already untying my apron. "For how long?"

"He never showed up for breakfast." Harper opened a lower cabinet, glanced in and moved on to the next cabinet. "And he's *never* late for breakfast."

I grabbed a thin sweater from a peg near the door and turned to the tiny woman still perched on her stool. "Greta, can you cover breakfast this morning?"

She straightened her back, spoon held in her hand like a scepter, and a firmness set into her face. "Course I can."

"Good," I said, then turned squarely to my sister. "And Lily can help."

Lily, who had paid little mind to any of the goings on, suddenly started. "I'll do what?"

Harper tugged on my arm and my jaw tightened. I turned to Lily. "You will help Greta serve breakfast to the guests this morning."

"You must be joking," she sputtered.

Greta slapped the spoon onto the counter and placed her fists firmly on her hips. "She'll muck it all up. I can do it alone."

"For once," I said, glaring at them both in turn, "can you two get through breakfast without killing each other?"

They both gaped at me speechless, like a pair of affronted trout as I followed Harper out the door.

***

Harper hurried off the porch, down the walkway, and onto the sidewalk. I followed behind, struggling to tug on my sweater and keep up with her long strides.

She motioned at me to hurry. "I've already got Angie searching behind the shops. Maybe he's feasting on salmon scraps from the fish guy or supplementing his diet with junk food crumbs from Shelby's."

"What can I do?"

Harper waved a hand toward the shops on the far side of Main Street. "Ask the shop owners if they've seen him."

"Okay."

"He's got to be around here somewhere." Her voice cracked at the end.

I placed a comforting hand on her shoulder.

"We'll find him. I promise."

She nodded and swallowed hard, choking down what I suspected was a lump of fear. I pulled her into a hug and she let it linger a moment before pushing me away. "Let's get going," she said, a mask of determination now on her face. "He's gonna be in big trouble when I find him."

I checked the first store on the road—the hardware store—but Trevor French hadn't seen Dewey all morning either.

The general store was next, and I looped out one door and through another. Ursula stood behind the counter, and she and Ryan chatted with Nick Christos, who glowed effortlessly like a modern Adonis.

"Shelby's got me jumping through hoops for this pageant." Nick ran a hand through his glossy hair. "Seems like a lot of work so far. I'm not even sure what to do, but Shelby just tells me to be quiet and look pretty, whatever that means."

"Sorry to interrupt," I said, ducking into their conversation, "but Harper can't find Mayor Dewey. Has anyone seen him this morning?"

Nick shook his head.

"I'm sure the little tyke will show up," Ryan said. "He's always hiding somewhere." Then he turned to Nick. "C'mon, I'll show you those vitamins you were asking about and you can tell me all about how much *work* the pageant is." He leveled a flat, disgruntled glare my way, which I pretended not to notice.

As Nick and Ryan drifted toward the pharmacy, Ursula said, "You know, now that I think of it, you might try the roof."

"The roof?"

"For Dewey. I've spotted him up there before, sitting on the cornice, surveying his domain. You know how he is."

"I didn't even know there was a roof."

Ursula cocked her head at my comment. "Every building has a roof."

"Right," I said. "I meant I didn't know there was roof access."

"Oh sure," Ursula said, as if this were common knowledge. "Hatch at the top of the second floor. Great view of the town and ocean. Table, chairs. Good times up there." She shook her head and chuckled at a memory. "I haven't been up there in ages. Bad knees."

"How can I reach it?" I asked.

Ursula pointed to a hall that led off the back of the store. "Through there. The latch can be a little tricky, so be careful."

"Thanks," I said, and darted down the hall.

My breath heaved after taking the stairs quicker than my fitness would allow. At the top of the stairwell there was a single rung of steps that led to a dusty metal hatch. A lit exit sign glowed next to the rungs with a few old cobwebs for company.

I took the rungs one by one and unfastened a latch that kept the hatch locked. An easy push and the hatch rotated to the side on its hinges. With my head poking through, I winced at the sudden daylight. When my eyes adjusted, I was dumbfounded. The roof sprawled the entire size of the store's footprint. A grimy glass-topped table and four sturdy metal chairs sat unused on the western side along with a wicker sofa and two wicker footstools. I finished my climb and took a gingerly step onto the roof, but it held firm beneath me. Behind me, facing east toward the sun, sat two reclining lounge chairs with a matching table in between.

I let out a deep sigh of relief. Rolled on his back atop one of the loungers lay Dewey, sunning his furry ginger underside, somewhat indecently, in the rays of the warm morning light.

"How did you even get up here?" I scanned the rooftop and quickly spotted the leaves of a tall tree skimming the brick railing on one side. The outstretched branches made a perfect bridge from the trunk to the roof.

Dewey twitched a foot as I approached, but kept his eyes shut, soaking in the sun. A low purr of pleasure escaped when I scratched the top of his head.

He was pliable after sunning and didn't protest when I slung him under an arm and descended the rungs—which was much easier said than done—closing the hatch behind me. I managed to escape the ordeal with only one minor scratch and a sweater covered in orange hairs.

"Oh, good," Ursula said as I appeared with Dewey in my arms, "you found him."

"He was warming his bits on one of those loungers."

"Cheeky boy." Ursula winked and ruffled the fur behind his ears. "Got to take advantage of the sun when we get it."

I leaned down and Dewey crawled from my arms. He sat squatly on the floor of the general store blinking in slow succession, but he didn't scurry off. A quick call and a relieved "I'll kill him" from Harper on the other end of the line told me everything would be okay.

As I waited for Harper to retrieve the mayor, my thoughts drifted to the dirty and dusty rooftop. I stole a look at Ryan, who counted pills methodically. When his glasses slipped down his nose, he used one index finger to push them back into place. I smiled. Maybe that rooftop mess could be the perfect private date retreat.

***

My plan that day was to meet Cabo in the town of Vista at noon. His request—or demand—for a secluded gig space meant I had to pull some strings, but hopefully this favor would keep him in our good graces. If things went well, maybe he'd even forget about the lawsuit against Starry Cove.

But I had some time to kill before then, and Greta's dodgy response to my question about the library that morning had me worried that she was up to something. And I didn't know this Moira very well, only that she was a librarian. *Librarians don't get into trouble, do they?* But with Greta involved… The last thing I needed was another Greta kerfuffle pulling me away from saving the town from financial oblivion.

I pulled into the library parking lot and sighed in relief as I parked my Prius next to the vintage blue Vespa Greta used to zip around town. At least she'd stowed it in a designated spot instead of on the lawn or upside down or some other odd configuration other than what was normal. I had to admit that was one good sign I wasn't expecting.

Inside, the library was quiet, save for a few voices carrying from the fiction stacks and a patron clacking away at a keyboard in one of the computer cubbies erected across from the checkout counter. There was no sign of Greta or Moira.

I spotted a mousy young woman behind the counter. Short and arrow-straight brown hair nearly covered her eyes, and her mouth was so small I couldn't imagine it could utter more than a peep. "Excuse me?" I asked.

The mousy woman gave a start and nearly dropped a pile of books stacked in her arms. "Y-yes?" she responded.

"Have you seen a wiry woman about this tall?" I held my hand up about four feet off the ground. "She might be here with Moira, the librarian."

At the mention of Moira, the woman's eyes grew large behind dangling strands of hair. She nodded toward a door at the far end of an array of comfy chairs that made up the reading area.

The door was propped open with a weighty volume pulled from a nearby set of encyclopedias. I decided to peek through the gap instead of barging in, expecting the worst. I imagined Greta ripping the pages from the other volumes and lathering them with her own spit to make some bizarre version of papier mâché. Or scribbling mathematical formulas on the walls with a bright orange crayon from atop three stacked tables.

I shook my head at the absurdity of it and eased the door open wider. Moira grunted as she heaved a round table into place on one side of a large room. I remembered her from previous visits to the library. She wore her brown hair in a tight bun and I guessed she was quite a few years younger than Greta, somewhere in her fifties, and another head taller. Greta followed closely behind Moira, tambourine jangling at her hip like a bell on a cat, and tossed a plain white cloth over the table then leveled it with her knotty hands, just like I'd taught her to smooth out the bedspreads at the Pearl.

"Just a few more," Greta said before spotting me in the doorway. "What the blazes are you doing here?"

The room was full of similar round tables with four chairs each, set up as if for an event.

"What's all this?" I asked, indicating the elaborate arrangement.

Moira brushed the dust off her hands. "It's for—"

"Nothing," Greta said. "It's for nothing. Why are you here?"

For one fleeting moment, I had almost thought Greta wasn't up to something. Almost. Now I sucked in through my teeth and leveled a stare at her. "I was in the neighborhood. Thought I'd pop in, ask how things went with Lily this morning. And to see where you've been spending all your time."

"Went swimmingly," Greta said. "I told her to shut her mouth and stay out of my way or I'd swat her bottom with my wooden spoon. Worked like a charm. So, now you know and off you go." She shooed at me with both hands, but I didn't move.

I walked my fingers over the top of the nearest table and let Greta squirm through the awkward silence. "Seems like there's something going on here."

"Just tell her," Moira said to Greta. "Then she'll go away."

Greta seemed to mull this over. The creases in her brow deepened and her mouth puckered. "Fine," she said, planting her fists on her hips. "Suit yourself. If you must know, we're setting up for a fundraiser."

"A fundraiser?"

"Don't act so surprised. Moira and I have been planning this for a long time."

"Sorry," I said, truly ashamed I'd thought the worst out of the gate. "I didn't expect you'd be so...

philanthropic."

"You told me to be more social. Well, here I am." Greta spread her hands out wide. "Socializing."

"I... That's great, Greta, really. I guess this explains why you've been busy at night. What is this fundraiser exactly?"

Greta and Moira exchanged wary glances and an unsaid agreement passed between them, then Moira nodded.

Greta turned back to me. "We're calling it Buncopalooza."

I blinked a few times. A bake sale or a book sale was more in line with what I was expecting. Maybe an art collection.

"The dice game?" I asked, incredulous.

"That's right," Moira said. "Bunco. Everyone loves it."

Although I'd never played, I remembered hearing about the party nights and ladies' get-togethers where bunco and free-flowing wine featured as the main draws. "I've heard it's pretty fun. When is this fundraiser?"

Greta grunted, clearly not wanting to share too much with me. "Tomorrow night."

I smiled knowingly. "So, that's why you asked for the night off."

Greta nodded, holding her chin up in defiance, as if I were going to reverse course.

"Well," I said, taking in the room at a glance, "I think it's wonderful. And I'm glad the two of you are doing it. Maybe I'll come by and play a round or two. Or I could help?"

"No, no," Greta said, waving her palms at me. "Not necessary. The guests at the Pearl will need you and we'll be just fine." She rounded on Moira. "Isn't that right?"

"Right, yes," Moira said. "We'll be fine. No need to trouble yourself."

"See," Greta said with a confident grin. "Everything's fine. I'll tell you all about it afterward." She shooed me to go once again.

"All right," I said, taking a step toward the exit. I leaned in and whispered to Greta. "I'm really glad you and Moira have become friends. And you don't need to be anxious about tomorrow. You'll do great."

"Uh, yeah, just my nerves," she said before shutting the door firmly behind me.

Six

I ROLLED INTO the familiar gravel parking lot of the Vista Tavern right at noon. A dented pickup truck with peeling blue paint and two beefy motorcycles were parked haphazardly near the front entrance. As he spotted me drive in, Cabo hopped out of his car, a garish red coupe, then stood waiting with one arm propped against his driver-side door.

"This place is perfect," he said giddily as we approached the windowless entrance. "Motorcycles, dark windows. There's even a train track running nearby."

"I told you." I grabbed the door handle, but paused and gave his outfit a once-over. Khaki shorts, boaters, and a gaudy Hawaiian shirt of bright pinks and greens. "Let me do the talking," I said. "Joe's not too friendly to outsiders."

Cabo nodded slyly, probably appreciative of my inside knowledge. The truth was that I didn't need Cabo to ruin this by opening his smarmy mouth. The Vista Tavern crowd was particular, and Cabo's approach would get him run out rather than welcomed.

We fell into darkness as I swung open the door to the dim interior. Joe, the owner, wiped down pint glasses behind the bar, and Gus and Hank, two grizzled regulars, sat at their usual barstools—the best spots to watch the dinky television installed in one upper corner. The white noise of an indistinct sporting event on television competed with the faint wailing of a guitar solo playing from a nearby radio. The entire place smelled of stale beer and sweat.

A chorus of greetings met me as the door shut behind us and the bright outside light faded.

"Poppy!" Joe, Gus, and Hank said in unison.

"Hey guys." I matched their genuine smiles.

Cabo stayed quiet, but peered around at the bar's interior, taking in the sight. Dingy, dark, secluded. Satisfaction shone behind a wide grin.

Gus swiveled on his stool and gave Cabo the same once-over I had. "This your, uh, fella?"

"What? No!" I took a step to the side, distancing myself from the band manager. "This is Cabo, he's a guest at my bed-and-breakfast."

A look of relief passed over all three of their faces.

"You two here for lunch?" Joe asked. "Today's special's pastrami."

Cabo's face turned an odd shade, something between green and white, but mixed with the orange of his tan, leathery skin.

"Don't let the place fool you," I whispered to him. "The food here is great. Especially the sandwiches."

He nodded and proffered a plastic smile for Joe.

"We'll take two," I said. "And two beers." I

motioned for Cabo to take a seat at the bar and I slid into the stool next to Hank. A few minutes later and Joe was back with our food. As the plates landed on the counter in front of us, I said, "We've got a proposal."

"Oh yeah?" Joe said, lifting an eyebrow.

"Cabo here manages a band and they're looking for a place to try out some new music."

Joe didn't twitch or give away any hint of interest or displeasure. "What kind of music?"

Cabo opened his mouth, but I kicked him under the bar.

"Rock," I said. "You may have heard of them. The Five Foxes?"

Hank tapped the bar with his finger. "Those the ones that sang 'Drunk on the Nile'?"

Cabo brightened. "Yes, it's—"

Another kick.

"That's the one," I said.

Joe picked up another glass and began to dry it with the towel hanging from his waist. "Don't know that I have the space for a whole band. Stage is a bit rickety, too."

"I'm sure it's—"

Kick.

"It's perfect," I said. "They're looking for something low-key, anyway."

Joe grunted with a nod. "When is this thing?"

I turned to Cabo.

"How about, ah," he began with a stutter then looked at me as if he wanted my help. I shrugged. He turned back to Joe. "How about the day after tomorrow?"

Joe's brow darkened. "Pretty short notice."

I waved a hand. "It's nothing fancy, just a little

background music for your patrons."

"Gets pretty rowdy here some nights," Gus said.

Hank side-eyed Cabo. "Shouldn't be nothin' your friend here can't handle."

Then Hank and Gus broke into peals of laughter and even Joe chuckled.

With the gig settled, we ate our sandwiches, and I caught up with Joe and the guys, sharing stories and lamenting over their favorite teams' losing records. As we prepared to go, Cabo excused himself outside, but I lingered back to say my goodbyes.

"What's with that guy, Poppy?" Gus asked. "Did you see his shoes?"

I sighed. "Yes. The thing is, he's threatening to sue Starry Cove and I'm trying everything to appease him so he'll back off."

Joe hefted a pint glass and began rubbing it furiously with his towel. "He giving you trouble?"

"Not me, personally, but the town's on edge. He could ruin us."

Hank leaned in and his voice was low. "We could straighten him out if you want."

Gus grunted in agreement.

"Thanks guys, but I need to work this out myself. Having the show here will be a big help."

Joe nodded. "Anything you need, just let us know."

Cabo waited in the parking lot and scurried over as I exited the bar. "You were right, that place is perfect. I couldn't have found better myself. It's just what we need."

"Good," I said, rounding on him. "And I hope you'll remember me going out of my way because Starry Cove has a lot to lose if you're still planning on suing."

Cabo scoffed. "It's not just about me. I have the whole band's interest to think of. I have an obligation."

I waved toward Vista Tavern. "I'm doing this for them, too."

He spread his hands as if there was nothing he could do. "I guess we'll see what the investigation finds."

As Cabo started his car and made a seven-point turn trying to get out of the lot, I wondered if what I'd done here was for nothing. All Cabo had to do was stop hinting at litigation and the others would probably forget about it, too, and all of this could just go away.

***

The moment I pushed through the door to Shelby's Diner that night, Lovie Newman squirmed in her seat.

I let out a heavy yawn as I reached the register. "Takeout tonight," I told Shelby.

"All right, dearie. Order when you're ready."

I stared at the menu board, deciding between the hamburger or the macaroni and cheese. Out of the corner of my eye, Lovie stared at me from her spot at the edge of the counter-level seating. Her fingers wiggled, then stopped, then wiggled again.

Letting out a heavy sigh, I turned her way. "Something you want to share with me, Lovie?"

"What? Oh," she said, feigning bewilderment. "I was just thinking about those band people staying at your house."

"Uh-huh."

"Do you know Bea Trotter?"

I inhaled deeply. Of course I knew Bea Trotter. She

was a town regular. Lovie was just setting up her story, but I was too exhausted from the long day to play her games. "Get on with it."

Lovie fussed, tucking a lock of her gray-blonde curls behind an ear. "Well, I heard from Bea that Pastor Basil mentioned to Georgia's sister that he's a big fan of the band."

"Okay, so?"

A twinge of a smile touched Lovie's lips. "And that he saw two of them through the doors of the community center in a heated conversation. *Heated.* Those were his exact words, according to Georgia's sister, who told Georgia, who then told Bea, who told me."

"What kind of heated conversation? When?"

Lovie wiggled again and I could tell she was savoring my undivided attention. "Gosh, I'm not sure, but I can ask Georgia to ask her sister to ask Pastor—"

I held up a palm and Lovie faltered. "Forget it," I said. Tonight, she wasn't worth the effort.

Shelby appeared through the swivel door that led to the kitchen. "Ready to order, dearie?"

I nodded. "The burger."

"Are you going to want fries with—wait. Is this for Ryan? Because I don't serve his fancy Scottish chips here, only fries, dearie."

"It's for me."

Shelby wrote my order on a ticket then tucked it into the wheel for the cook in the back. "Have you got Ryan on board for the Mista Vista Pageant yet?"

"I asked him yesterday. He was a little squirrelly, but he came around eventually. I think he has a pretty good chance, too. He's the most well-rounded. Good-looking, educated, humble."

"I'll admit, dearie," Shelby said, "he's got that sexy accent going for him, but no one'll be able to see Ryan's personality through the blinding glow of Nick's halo."

With Nick in the competition, it would be hard to sway any of the judges, especially Veronica Valentine. I already had a few strikes against me in her book, so Ryan and I would have to lay on the charm pretty thick. "It'll be good fun, no matter what," I said. "Plus, it's for a good cause."

"Of course, dearie." Shelby tried to hold back a grin. Nick was a ringer and she knew it. "What about you, Lovie? Is our deputy going to grace the stage?"

Lovie shook her curls and took on a haughty air. "Unfortunately, Todd... I mean, the deputy, will be on patrol that day. As you know, he's the arm of the law in this area, and he has a duty to the town."

"Uh-huh," I mumbled, trying not to roll my eyes. "Glad to have the deputy there in case one of the shelter puppies goes on a rampage."

Lovie sniffed. "You of all people should know that things can get dangerous around here, since the deputy is still investigating *your* guest's death at our community center."

"And how exactly is that investigation going?"

Lovie's eyes went wide. "How should *I* know?"

I leaned in. "You know when a dog poops on a lawn three miles away. You know how many drinks a person's had on Saturday and how much they tithe on Sunday. You know about everything the split second after it happens. So, tell me what Deputy Todd has found out."

Her back stiffened with every statement and her curls

bristled.

Shelby stepped over, stopping in front of Lovie and me. "Don't bother, dearie. If there was anything to spill, half the town would know it by now. Looks like you'll just have to wait."

Seven

TO MY SURPRISE, Lily joined Greta and me in the kitchen without prompting the next morning. "Everything all right?" I asked her.

She lifted a mug and waved it in the air without a word, and I knew exactly what she meant. I lifted my own mug of hot coffee and let my eyelids close as I savored the deep, rich aroma.

Voices drifted into the kitchen from the dining room. The guests must have taken their seats and were chatting before breakfast would be served.

"How's it looking?" I asked Greta.

Greta, perched on her stool, snatched two eggs in each hand from the carton nearby and in one swift motion, had cracked all four. Their oozy innards hit the skillet with a steamy hiss. "Fine."

"What are you making?"

"Eggs."

I put down my mug. "Are you mad at me?"

"No."

"Don't bother," Lily said from the kitchen table. "The old hag barely said two words to me yesterday. Just let her concoct whatever potion she's brewing and sit and enjoy your coffee like me."

Greta guffawed audibly. "For once she speaks some sense. Just let me work and stay out of my hair."

I held up my hands in deference. "Fine, fine." I eased into the seat next to Lily.

"But before you get comfy," Greta said, "I need that casserole dish from the second cabinet. Don't know why you insist on storing it so high only a giraffe could reach it."

I eased myself back up with a groan. "It's not my fault you have the height and arm span of a child."

As I reached into the cabinet, a shout came from the dining room.

"What was that?" Lily asked.

Another loud voice boomed through the swivel door. "I guess you finally got what you wanted!"

"That was Cherry." I quickly placed the heavy glass casserole dish on the counter. Pushing through the swivel door, I found Cherry in tears.

"I only said I was excited to play guitar." Dutch looked around at the other faces in confusion.

"Yeah," Cherry sneered. "Just what you wanted."

"Come on, Cherry…" Hips shook his head.

"Hey, sweetheart," Wings said in a mocking tone, "you got exactly what you wanted, too, so pipe down."

Dee's brow furrowed. "Don't call her that. I'll—"

"You'll what?" Wings asked, urging Dee on. "Don't you get it? She's got *everything*, man."

Cherry shot up, scooting back her chair with her legs.

"I never wanted this, but you refuse to let it go, Wings."

"Me?" Wings said, fuming. "I'm not the one who sold us out to the papers."

Cabo held out his hands. "All right, let's all just calm down."

"I am calm!" Cherry shouted, then whipped her napkin onto the table and stormed out of the room, her red hair sailing behind her. A moment later, the front door slammed.

Wings shrugged. "Why is she still here, anyway?"

"Chill, man," Slomo said, shaking his head.

I composed myself as the band members settled back down. "I'll just... I'll go see how she is."

I eased open the front door, hoping she hadn't run off.

"Leave me alone," Cherry said from the wooden bench on the porch. She was turned away from the door, huddled in on herself.

"Cherry?"

"Oh, Poppy, it's you." She straightened and wiped away a tear from her pale cheek. "Sorry you had to hear that."

"It's okay."

She chuckled scornfully. "No, it's not."

"You're right," I said, taking a seat next to her on the bench. "You lost your husband. How could that ever be okay?"

Cherry just shook her head. "It's more than that."

"Do you mean what Wings said? About you getting what you wanted?"

"Wings." She let out a derisive scoff. "He's as mad as ever, so don't listen to a thing he says."

"Why not?"

Cherry turned to face me directly. "Did you know Wings tried a solo career? Wanted to leave the band and go off on his own."

I shook my head, even though I knew the question was rhetorical.

"Wings always hated Tango. Always. Hated him to the bone. Hated him so much that he left the band. Well, that solo career bombed. Hard. I guess he thought because he writes a lot of songs for the band that he'd magically become a star. But he forgot that Tango was the face of this band, and if you don't have a face, you've got nothing. Wings doesn't have the face. So, yeah, it bombed."

"And he holds that against you?"

"He'd hold it against anyone with ties to Tango. If Tango went left, Wings went right. He'd disagree with Tango, even if Tango made sense. It was like a reflex for him. He calls me Yoko. Can you believe that? Accuses me of breaking up the band."

"Seems like there's a lot of turbulence."

"It's not me, though," she said. "It's Wings who's caused all the problems. I just pushed Tango to achieve his potential. I guess Wings resented that, but I'm no Yoko." Tears began to stream down her cheeks and she buried her face in her hands. "It's not my fault Tango got into drugs. And we all drink. It's the scene, the lifestyle, you know?"

Having never been a rock star, I did not know, but I'd heard enough stories of musician overdoses to get the picture. "How did the others feel about Tango?"

Cherry chewed on her bottom lip before responding. "I guess there was some kind of trouble."

"Trouble?"

"Yeah," she said. "Disagreements. Fights. It was constant."

Fights. That sounded bad. I thought back to the scene at the community center right before Tango was electrocuted. The others had all ignored him, hadn't they? Or were Cherry and Tango too wrapped up in each other to have noticed? "Cherry," I began in a soft voice, "do you think these fights could have led to something more serious? Maybe bad enough that one of them would hurt Tango?"

Cherry wiped another tear from her red, swollen eyes and her voice took on a more serious tone. "You mean… You think one of them could have caused this?"

"I don't know. I'm just trying to find out the truth."

Her face darkened, and she stared at me more intently. "You think one of the band members sabotaged the equipment." She went silent, turning in on herself as her own words sank in. The idea that one of those closest to her could have killed her husband must have been devastating. She looked at me once again, this time more hopeful. "Why do you care so much?"

I wanted to admit it was because losing Tango was such a tragedy. Or that he deserved the truth. That my humanity ran so deep that I felt it my mission to vindicate him. But I told the truth instead. "Cabo's threatening to sue the town for faulty electrical. He could ruin us. I thought it may be possible that this was something else."

Cherry nodded, her lips now tightened as if she too was convinced Tango's death was no accident. "Wings could have done it. I don't see it in the others, and definitely not Dee."

"Why not Dee?"

She averted her eyes at my question. "I just don't. He's too nice." Her words were decisive, clearly meant to put an end to that questioning.

I didn't push it.

"What about Dutch?" I asked, changing the subject. "What did you mean when you said he finally got what he wanted?"

She twisted one of the loose threads of her sweater between two fingers, then let out a heavy sigh. "I shouldn't have shouted at him." She shook her head at the memory. "He's always wanted to be in the band. He's been the roadie for as long as I can remember, but it's hard to sit there and listen to his excitement when my husband is dead." She began to cry again, softer this time.

I placed a hand on her back and she leaned in, using my shoulder to rest her cheek. "You don't have to stay here, Cherry. You should be with family right now."

She bolted upright and wiped away the last few of her remaining tears. "I can't."

She was so adamant, and I couldn't understand why. "It's obvious that being around the band is difficult for you. Why not just go home?"

Her words were clear. "It's not that, Poppy. It's Cabo. I've seen the numbers—he's running the band into the ground. Tango was too strung out to understand, but now it's my stake, and my say in the band is the only thing keeping Cabo from ruining them all."

***

Later that morning, I retreated to Angie's bakery to escape the maddening buzz of the band's morning practice session.

"What exactly is Bun Co.?" Harper asked through a mouthful of cinnamon roll.

"It's bunco," I corrected from across the table.

"Oh, Harper, it's so much fun." Angie's cheeks shone with rosiness, and a twinkle sparkled in her eyes. "There are dice and you count them out and then you rotate tables and there's a doll or something—I forget what it's for—and there're treats and all sorts of goodies. It's just... It's just so much fun." She scurried behind the counter and began slapping a ball of dough against the marble countertop with a hearty giggle. "So much fun."

"And you said Greta was organizing this?" Harper's voice held a hint of suspicion.

"And Moira, the librarian."

Angie slapped the dough again with a smack and began to knead, putting all her weight behind the movement. "We're going, right? We should go. I can bring samples of my new sourdough and do a test study. Everyone will like that. Everyone loves samples. How many people do you think will be there?"

I took a long drag from my coffee mug, letting Angie knead out all of her excitement. "I don't know, but there were a lot of tables set out."

"Probably a big group. Do you think Greta's looking for caterers? I'm sure Shelby would be up for it." Angie reached under the counter and brought out a notebook and pencil. She began to scribble, mumbling to herself before erasing, then scribbled something else with an approving nod.

"Not sure," I said. "I can ask if you want, but the event is tonight. Will there be time?"

Angie tapped her lip with the pencil. "No, probably not. Better stick to my sourdough samples. Three variations. Maybe four, I think."

"Excuse me," Harper said, "but have you both forgotten that the town is in imminent danger of being sued to the gills by a leathery snake in a tacky Hawaiian shirt?"

Angie frowned. "Oh, right."

"And since Poppy's band has closed down the community center, I've had to jump through some serious hoops to make new arrangements for the Mista Vista Pageant. Arrangements that included a lot of concessions to the county organizers in order to keep the contract, by the way."

"What kind of concessions?" I asked.

"Like it's going to be outdoors on Main Street, and Starry Cove will have to pick up a lot of the organizing slack."

"And by 'Starry Cove' you mean you?"

Harper nodded. "And there's more." She averted her eyes. "I maybe sorta kinda promised we'd have live music."

"Live music?" Angie repeated. "But where are you going to find a band at such short…" Her eyes darted my way. "Oh."

I stared Harper down.

Harper returned my stare with a mega-watt smile and batted her long brown lashes. "C'mon, Poppy. It's a great idea. The band will get some practice in, the adoration of the crowd, and the town is willing to pay."

"I don't know… I can't imagine Cabo would go for something as public as the Mista Vista Pageant. I just got them a gig at the Vista Tavern because he wanted something small and low-key."

"Just ask him, will ya? There is a few thousand bucks in it for them if they agree. And it would get me out of a real bind."

"All right," I said. "But don't be surprised if the answer is no, and then you'll have to get Angie's cousin's garage band to play."

"Oof," Angie said with a grunt. "They're terrible."

Harper grimaced. "So, what's this about the Vista Tavern?"

I told Angie and Harper about Cabo's request, and about how the Vista Tavern was the perfect spot for them to acclimate themselves to their new material.

"Good," Harper said. "They can get some practice in before the pageant."

"And we can have a night out," I said.

Angie clutched her apron in both hands like a security blanket. "I'm not going there. I've heard that place is pretty rough."

"Aren't you buddies with the owner, Poppy?"

"Yes. And it's not rough. I mean, it's not dangerous. It's sort of dirty and dark. But not rough."

"What about me?" Harper tapped the rainbow headband that held back her dark brown curls.

"They aren't bad people. If you're friends of mine, you're friends of theirs. And it will give me an opportunity to take a close look at Cabo's business dealings."

"Business dealings?" Harper asked.

"Cherry told me this morning that Cabo's bleeding the band dry. Mismanagement."

Harper snorted and slapped a skinny hand on the table. "I knew it! That scoundrel is only after money. No wonder he was so eager to sue us."

Angie looked to me. "So does that mean Tango's death was an accident and Cabo's just making up a reason to sue Starry Cove?"

"I'm not sure," I said. "But Cherry also said Wings could be capable of anything when it came to Tango."

"Gosh…"

"This band sounds like a steaming pile of you-know-what. I'm surprised they ever got an album out at all."

"There's more," I said. "I'm headed to the church after this to talk to Pastor Basil. Lovie mentioned that he may have seen something going on at the community center."

Harper straightened in her chair. "Something fishy?"

"Maybe. I have to ask him. I don't really trust Lovie's fourth-hand gossip."

"I wouldn't either," Angie said with a groan. "Yesterday she told me that Mrs. Perez's poodle Pinkie had died, but then I saw Mrs. Perez with her poodle, whose fur had been *dyed* bright pink."

"But sometimes Lovie's partly right." I shoved the remainder of my cinnamon roll into my mouth and headed for the door. "I just need to find out what part."

***

As I approached the non-denominational Fellowship of the Faith church farther down Main Street, I spied Pastor Basil in his wool sweater and Birkenstock sandals, long hair pulled back into a ponytail at the base of his neck, observing some goings-on along the side wall. Ethan MacKenzie stood in the flower beds lining the sides of the church tugging on a vine of ivy that had grown up along the cobblestone wall. With each tug, a shower of leaves and detritus fell down upon his head.

"You've got to pull harder, man." Pastor Basil's softly spoken words barely registered between the young man's grunts.

"What's this?" I asked, taking a spot next to the pastor on the garden pathway.

"Ivy," the pastor said. "I'm fond of weeds, ya dig? But under all God's creation, I don't get the purpose of ivy. Blows my mind how it bores right into the stone."

Ethan's knee-high waders stepped roughly through the flowerbeds, and his pants, shirt, and gloves were covered with tiny specks of dead and disengaged ivy.

"Don't crush the bulbs, son. They're sleeping under your feet."

"Is this more volunteering? I saw Ethan at Ursula's the other day, too."

"Mm-hmm. Rolled through the church doors an hour ago and asked if there was anything he could do. I said, 'Groovy, man. Even yard work is the Lord's work.'"

"Pastor, I was hoping I could talk to you in private?"

There was only a slight raise to the bushy eyebrows behind his circular glasses. He was probably used to this sort of request. "Sure, Poppy. Let me finish up with Ethan and I'll be right in. I'm a mellow fella, but those cloppers of his are trampling the irises and I should provide a guiding hand."

The resonance of a male voice singing octaves met me as I passed the threshold. Dutch stood near the pulpit, practicing the scales. With the church's acoustics, his voice wasn't half bad. He stopped as I approached.

"You've got a lovely voice, Dutch."

His cheeks reddened. "Thanks. I've been practicing hard. Don't want to let the guys down."

"I'm sure you won't."

"You won't tell them about this, will you?" He indicated the church. "They'd laugh if they knew."

I waved a hand. "Of course not. I think it's admirable that you want to impress the guys. This is a great opportunity."

"The guys, yeah." A single loose thread hung from Dutch's faded T-shirt. The image of the band's name had long since faded over time. He twisted the thread between his thumb and forefinger. "Do you... Do you think Greta likes a man who can sing?"

The thought of this nice man pining after prickly Greta was beyond me, but I guess it's all in the eye of the beholder. "I'm not sure, Dutch. But it can't hurt." I gave him a cheerful wink.

He smiled awkwardly in return and twisted the thread harder.

"Are you excited about the show tomorrow? I'm familiar with the venue, and it should be a lot of fun."

"Uh, yeah." Twist. "It'll be my first time on stage with the band. Other than switching out their guitars, I mean." Twist, twist.

I gave him my best, most confident smile. "You have a great voice and you know all the songs. I've heard you all in practice. You'll do fine."

"I've been taking lessons in L.A., too." Twist. "Now that the moment is here, I'm shaking. Not sure if it's from excitement or nerves."

"Either way," I said, "the band is lucky to have you and you're going to have a wonderful time. I'll be there to support you."

Twist. "Thanks, Poppy."

"But who's going to set up for you guys? There's still setting up to do, right?"

"Oh, that'll be me still. And the other guys help sometimes, too, even Cabo."

Dutch had stopped twisting his loose thread, and I assumed his nerves had at least settled enough for me to try my next question. "What about the day Tango died? Who did the set up that day?"

His face fell in an instant and I regretted bringing it up. I cursed Harper under my breath, but I had to help the town in whatever way I could.

"I did the set up that morning. Most of it. The guys sometimes wrangle their own cords."

"And you didn't notice anything... funny?"

He shook his head. "Nothing."

I thought on this a moment. Nothing out of the ordinary with the equipment that day? Then how could a system that could handle Mrs. Perez's gaudy dancing bears fail right at that moment?

"There is one thing," Dutch said. "And I don't feel right even saying it, but..."

I tilted my head, urging him to finish.

"It's just that Hips had a lot to gain from Tango, um..." Twist. "From Tango dying."

"Do you think Hips could be responsible for...?"

"No, no." Dutch waved his hands. "I'm not saying that at all." He took a deep breath. "It's just that Hips has been getting sloppy."

"Sloppy?"

"Yeah, dropped chords. Real unfocused. Hips shares

a lot with me—we're good friends—but I think he was having trouble with what he was doing."

"What kind of trouble?"

Twist. "I suppose it wouldn't hurt to tell you..."

"Tell me what?"

Dutch took a deep breath. "Hips has trouble with his fingers. Arthritis or something. It's been getting bad for a while now. He hasn't told the others, so don't say anything. He confided in me 'cause we're close. So, all I'm saying is maybe he wanted—needed—to try something different."

"I see."

Dutch dropped his head with a look of shame on his face.

I placed a hand on his shoulder. "It's okay, Dutch. You're not accusing anyone."

He nodded, face still downcast.

"You know," I said in a cheerier tone, "I think Greta *did* mention once that she likes men who sing."

His face lit up. "Yeah?"

"Yeah, and she carries that tambourine everywhere."

"She does?"

I nodded emphatically and his hopeful smile made me smile.

Pastor Basil approached down the aisle, so I left Dutch with that glimmer of hope.

"Sorry for that wait, Poppy." He pressed his hands together as if in prayer. "How may I be of service?"

I guided Pastor Basil away from Dutch, giving the stout man a farewell wave. "I wanted to ask you about something Lovie Newman mentioned."

"Oh," he said with a grin, "must be of vital

importance."

"It's not gossip," I assured him. "It has to do with something you saw the night before Tango McColl died. Lovie said you saw two of my guests at the community center."

Pastor Basil squinted, then pulled off his rimless, circular glasses. He rubbed them clean with the edge of the tie-dyed shirt under his wool sweater. "Well, let me think." He placed his glasses softly on the bridge of his nose. "Two men were skulking in the shadows outside the building, trying to hide, like. I got a weird vibe, ya dig? The way you'd hide from the fuzz."

"Did you recognize who they were? Which one of my guests?"

"The light was dim. Hmm. Some guy was flailing his arms around."

I leaned in. "Like fighting?"

"No, man, just real animated. I remember the dude wore some hip threads."

"Hip threads?"

"Like, a loud shirt. Bright pink and yellows. Even at night I could see that."

I set my jaw. *Cabo.*

"What about the other man?" I asked.

"Now that fella was also talking, but he just leaned against the wall, even while Loud Shirt flailed like a maniac. This guy was cool as a cucumber. Real tall. Barely moved."

I knew who that was, too. Only one of my guests would be that low-key while Cabo flapped around like a chicken: Slomo.

"Could you hear what they were saying?"

"Nah, I was too far. But after a minute Loud Shirt left and Cool Cucumber just stood there alone, leaning against the wall."

The door of the church opened and Shelby appeared in the aisle. Her voice boomed through the space. "Time to clear out, dearies." She swiveled a finger over her head as if to round up the three people in the church. Nick Christos stood a few feet behind her and kept his eyes down, staying squarely out of Shelby's way.

"What's going on?" I asked.

Dutch didn't wait for an answer. He scurried past me and was out the door in an instant.

"You've got to skedaddle, too, dearie," Shelby said to me. "I'm afraid I've got this space reserved for Nick's Mista Vista practice." She put her hands firmly on the hips of her diner uniform. "With the community center closed, this is the only available space. I've got a few precious minutes between the breakfast and lunch rush and, well, you've got to go." She clasped a firm hand on my arm and guided me to the exit. "Maybe you should spend some time prepping Ryan, dearie. He's gonna need it." She grinned as the church door closed in my face.

***

Shelby's needling aside, some time with Ryan would not go amiss, and with an hour or two of free time, I decided I would stop in for an early lunch and pageant prep.

Voices from the backyard drew me to the gate at Ryan's house, and I popped through balancing takeout from Shelby's diner in my arms.

Ryan's eyes lit up as I rounded the corner into the yard. "Is that a burger and chips I smell?"

"Thought you two might be hungry. I see Ethan's working up an appetite." I nodded toward Ethan, who stood among a heap of debris below a half-built redwood gazebo. His shoulders were already slumped in defeat.

"Aye," Ryan said. "Asked if putting the old gazebo together would earn him volunteer hours. I said no."

I cocked my head.

Ryan continued, "Instead I offered to pay him to put it together. You know, learn the value of hard work. That sort of thing."

"Ah, so he's doing it for the cold, hard cash?"

"Aye. And with all that experience building birdhouses, he might just have a chance."

"How much are you paying him?"

"That there's the genius of it. He gets paid upon completion." Ryan winked at me slyly. "But you're not here to watch Ethan put that contraption together."

"No," I admitted, setting the food down on a nearby table. "I thought we might do a little preparation for the Mista Vista pageant."

Ryan hushed me, sparing a quick glance at Ethan, who was pounding away with a hammer and paying us no mind. "He might hear you."

"You haven't told him yet?"

Ryan bit into a French fry. "Not yet. I'll lose all my cool dad cred once he finds out."

"You don't know that."

"He's a teenage boy, Poppy. Everything I do is embarrassing."

"Then when are we going to prepare?"

Ryan shrugged. "What's to prepare, anyway?"

"I have an idea. Remember that date you wanted in

exchange for entering the pageant?"

He raised a single eyebrow behind his glasses.

"Why don't I meet you at the pharmacy after work in two days?"

"Okay, but why in two days?"

"Because tonight is Greta's Buncopalooza and tomorrow we're going to the band's gig in Vista."

"Ah, I'd forgotten."

I waved Ethan over to eat, and he took a seat by his father before digging into lunch. "You've been doing a lot of hard work around town," I said.

Ethan mumbled in the affirmative, mouth full of cheeseburger.

"Better be careful or else you'll end up stiff and achy."

"Not young chaps like Ethan," Ryan said, slapping the boy on the back. "Made of Scottish steel."

Ethan rolled his eyes and shrugged the hand off, then picked up his takeout container and disappeared to the other side of the yard.

"See? Embarrassing." Ryan shook his head and took a bite out of his burger.

"I suppose he could always take something to dull the pain," I said. "A pill or something. For joints. Joint pain. Something to help with pain in the joint area. Like the hands, fingers. Finger pain, you know?"

Ryan stopped chewing and eyed me suspiciously.

"I'm just curious," I said. "Greta's getting on in years and I, uh, thought she might…"

Ryan's eyes narrowed to slits.

"Okay, fine," I said, heaving a sigh. "I saw one of my guests ask you about pills for pain he had in his fingers and I wanted to ask you about it. And before you say anything, I'm not snooping. He said it all within earshot of me."

"Mm-hmm."

"So?" I urged. "What can you tell me?"

He put down his burger and dabbed the corners of his mouth with a paper napkin, then cleared his throat. "Osteoarthritis is a common condition that affects the joints, making them swell and stiffen, and it can be quite painful. Treatment includes oral pain relievers."

"How painful?"

Ryan blinked. "Why does that matter?"

I chewed at my lip. "Would it be debilitating pain or just kind of annoying?"

Ryan shrugged. "It varies from case to case."

"Would it affect your mental state?"

"Mental state… What are you getting at? Does this have anything to do with the death of that singer?" Ryan clicked his tongue. "I'm sure Deputy Todd told you to stay out of it, but I'm also sure you'd ignore him."

I turned away sheepishly. "I need to look down every avenue, and this seemed as good a lead as any."

We finished our burgers in silence, but that only gave me time to wonder about Hips' arthritis diagnosis. *Just how bad could the pain get? Could it drive him to kill?*

"You know," Ryan said, as if reading my mind, "it's a big leap from medically treatable arthritis to murder. I'm not sure where you're going with this, but be careful. For me, okay? Be careful."

Eight

BUNCOPALOOZA WAS UPON us, and Harper, Angie, and I gathered in my kitchen before the event. Lily, whole-heartedly disinterested, sat at the table reading while Angie fussed with excitement.

"I brought my own dice," Angie said. "Do you think they'll have dice, or do we need to bring our own? I've got extra for both of you if we do. And the bread." She patted the insulated bag slung over her shoulder. "I hope Greta doesn't mind if I set it out. Everyone's feedback would be so helpful in perfecting grandpa Hauser's recipe."

Harper waved a dismissive hand. "She won't care about your bread. I'm just worried she's up to something."

"Don't be so distrustful," I said. "Greta's found a friend and a hobby and I think it's great."

Lily closed her book with an exasperated sigh. "This bunco game sounds like it's for sad single women and bored housewives. You just toss dice over and over?"

"Oh no," Angie said. "It's more than that. You keep track and then you move from table to table and—"

"Why don't you join us, Lily?

Harper shot me a glare and mouthed "No."

Lily regarded me flatly. "Don't be absurd."

"C'mon, it'll get you out of the house."

"I am quite comfortable here, enjoying any and all time I have without that horrible old woman constantly skulking about and muttering like a crazed lunatic."

"Okay." I leaned against the counter and folded my arms. "If you don't think you can win, it's no trouble. You can stay here with Cabo. He's been very friendly toward you."

The haughtiness on her face faded to one of dread. "No one mentioned bunco was a competitive sport."

"Game, sport, whatever," I said. "Are you coming or not?"

Lily stood. "Fine. I'll get my coat."

As she left the kitchen, Harper bolted to my side. "Why'd you have to invite her? She's *awful*. I'd rather jab hot pokers in my eye than spend the night with her around."

Angie chewed on her bottom lip. "Maybe it won't be so bad."

"Look," I whispered. "Lily's got to get out of the house and start experiencing life."

Harper groaned.

"If she gets too comfortable, I'm worried she'll never leave."

The clack of Lily's designer heels signaled her return. "Shall we?"

The drive to the Vista Library was spent debriefing

on what I'd learned at the church that day from Pastor Basil.

Angie leaned in between the front seats of my car. "What do you think Cabo and Slomo were talking about?"

"I don't know, but Pastor Basil made it clear that Cabo seemed agitated or excited about something."

Harper seemed sure she knew what it was about. "Probably plotting how to defraud the town and pocket the money for themselves. This can't be a coincidence. Did Pastor Basil see them inside at all?"

"No, just outside."

"Doesn't mean they didn't do it," Harper said. "I don't trust any of those guys. They've all got something to gain from taking the town down. And what about Hips and his dodgy fingers? If his guitar-playing days were numbered…"

Angie fretted. "It's hard to imagine anyone could hurt another person, but that does seem suspicious. Hips had a lot to gain."

The conversation ended as we pulled into the library. The lot was nearly full, with only a few spots left open, one of which I pulled into and we tumbled out of the car.

"Gosh," Angie said. "Buncopalooza must have been well advertised. I didn't see anything in Starry Cove, though."

Harper tugged at her rainbow scarf. "Maybe it's just a Vista thing and we aren't supposed to be here?"

The library door was shut, but Moira sat just outside on a chair. She wore her hair in a bun, and an oversized green cardigan draped over her slight form. The long khaki skirt was the final touch to ensure no one would mistake her as anything other than a librarian. She greeted us as we approached. "Good evening. Are you here for the special event?"

We stepped into the lights that shone from the overhead cover.

"Oh, hi Poppy," Moira said. She glanced at Harper and Angie, who stood just behind me, but lingered on Lily, who stayed a few feet back. "I didn't know you were a twin."

"What?" I asked, surprised by this strange statement. I followed Moira's gaze to Lily. "Oh, no. My sister and I just look a lot alike."

Moira grunted. "That'll be ten—"

The door to the library burst open. Greta rushed out, her gray dress billowing around her. She rushed at Moira and the librarian's eyes went big. "No, Moira," Greta said through great heaves, coming to a halt just before she would have fallen into the woman. "I'll take care of these four."

Greta motioned us inside and we followed.

"What was that about?" I asked her. "I thought you were about to tackle Moira."

Greta waved me off. "Nothing, nothing."

We entered the large room in the back where the tables had been set up earlier. The room buzzed with the energy of the dozens of women who filled the space. A large group lingered around what appeared to be a refreshments table, which I pointed out to Angie. Others sat at the various tables, chatting with one another. All had drinks in their hands or at their side, some mixed concoctions with dainty straws, or bottled beverages like beer or wine coolers.

Harper leaned in close to my ear. "Is *that* allowed at the library?"

I frowned. "Maybe after hours?"

Greta scanned the room and hustled over to an empty table in a dim corner, then waved us over. The deep green tablecloth made the corner even darker.

"Good." Lily took the chair in the farthest corner. "These fluorescent lights are abominable."

"Oh, Greta," Angie said, catching the old woman's attention. She pulled three sourdough loaves from her insulated bag. "I was wondering if I could put these out and maybe ask your attendees for some feedback? I've been working on an old recipe for—"

"Do whatever you want," Greta said. "Just don't make a fuss. You know the rules of the game?"

Angie nodded emphatically. "Yes, I love bunco. It's one of my favorite—"

And with that, Greta rushed off.

"She's always so charming," Harper said. "Really, a wonderful hostess."

"I didn't expect so many people," I said. "This should be a great fundraiser."

Harper leaned in with her elbows square on the table. "What exactly is Greta raising funds for?"

"I… I didn't ask. The library, I suppose. But I think it's great that she's out and social, don't you?"

Harper's eye twitched, and she grunted in response.

A tinkling of glass hushed the crowd and Angie waved a pudgy hand to quiet us. "I think they're starting."

As the players took their seats, I spotted Moira over their heads, standing at the far end of the room as if about to make a speech. Only a few lingering laughs and voices cut through the air. I couldn't see Greta anywhere.

Moira tapped a fork against her glass again to quiet the final chatter. "Thank you, thank you. I want to welcome you all to the first ever Buncopalooza."

A round of clapping took over the room, Angie included. I joined in, and Harper slapped one hand against another at least twice. Lily remained stoic, hands clasped in her lap.

"You've all been briefed on the rules," Moira continued.

I caught Angie's eye and shook my head nervously before she whispered, "Don't worry, it's easy."

Moira continued. "There will be twenty-four rounds, with a twenty-minute break after the second round of sixes. With thirty-six players, we have three groups: A, B, and C. Make sure you are rotating within the appropriate group. We've made it easy by using different colored table clothes so A is pink, B yellow, and C green. Just a reminder that once play begins, withdrawals will not be reimbursed and all pledges are final."

I looked again to Angie in confusion. She shrugged.

"All right," Moira said, "I know you're all eager to get started, so I won't keep you waiting." Moira turned to a pink table at the front, where four middle-aged women sat with smiles beaming on their faces. A pair of over-sized hot pink fuzzy dice sat like a centerpiece in the middle, and a quick glance found corresponding colored dice at one of the tables for each color. "Head table A, you may ring us in when you're ready."

The players turned in unison back to their own tables, and I did the same, squaring up with Angie to my right, Harper to the left, and Lily across. A stack of what appeared to be scorecards sat near the center, with four pens and three white dice. A stand in the middle read C3.

"Ok," Angie said, hurriedly. "Everyone grab a scorecard and write your name. I'll start when they ring the bell. Here's how it works. We start with rolling ones. Each person rolls the dice until they don't roll any ones, then it moves clockwise to the next person. Harper and I are one team, Poppy and Lily the other."

Lily raised an eyebrow at me.

Sounds from other tables already threatened to overtake Angie's soft voice, but she continued. "I'll mark off how many ones each team scores. We keep going around like that until—"

The ringing of the bell chimed through the room. The voices at other tables rose and the clatter of rolling dice began.

"Oh my gosh," Angie said, flailing her pudgy hands. "Okay, okay. I'm going to get us started." She grabbed the three dice with her left hand and held a pen in her right. After a jostle, she threw the dice onto the table. Three, four, one. "That's one point for Harper and me, so I roll again."

Angie's second roll showed no ones, so she handed the dice to me. I, too, scored one point before failing to roll another one and the dice passed to Harper.

Harper rolled two, six, three. She frowned. "I thought this would be more fun."

"Sorry, Harper," Angie said. "Sometimes you roll a big goose egg. You'll have more chances."

Harper passed the dice to Lily. She sighed and rolled them casually. One, one, five.

"That's two points for Poppy and Lily." Angie

scribbled the marks on a scorepad.

In contrast with Angie's frantic rolling, Lily took her time retrieving the dice. She cupped them in her hands and gave them a half-hearted jiggle before letting them fall to the table. One, one, one.

"Bunco!" Angie popped up from her chair. She beamed at us and clapped her hands together, all while twittering excitedly.

Murmurs of shock drifted through the room as all eyes turned our way.

"We have a bunco already," Moira announced through the microphone with a twinge of surprise in her voice. She snatched up the green fuzzy dice and carried it to our table. Angie pointed to Lily, and Moira handed her the plushy dice. "Congratulations."

Lily took the dice reluctantly and placed it on the table with a sneer as if to disassociate herself with such a gaudy item.

Angie sat back down. "Lily gets to score a bunco on her card and that's also twenty-one points for her and Poppy."

"What?" Harper gaped. "Twenty-one? How're we supposed to beat that with piddly ones and twos?"

"It's a long game," Angie said. "For now, Lily will carry the fuzzy dice with her, but that could change."

Lily blinked. "Excuse me, did you say I have to carry this *thing* around?"

"Only until someone else gets a bunco. We should keep going. Lily, it's still your turn."

Another roll. One, two, six.

Angie marked the score.

One, one, two.

Harper scowled. "Unbelievable. She didn't even want to come."

Lily appeared unperturbed. Just as she rolled again—no ones—the bell sounded. Murmurs and scuffling behind me indicated everyone had stood up. The room was a mess, with bodies going every which way.

"That's the end of the round." Angie studied the score sheet closely and mumbled while she tallied the final scores.

"What do we do now?" I asked.

"For you and Lily, write a W on your scorecard for that round. You'll both move up to the table labeled C2."

"What about us?" Harper asked.

"We'll write a L on our scorecard and stay here at the lowest table."

Harper grumbled. "L for loser?"

Angie ignored her. "Next round is twos. It's the same thing." She shooed Lily and me away, adding, "Just ask your table for help if you don't understand."

After much searching, Lily and I found table C2 closer to the center of the room, mostly by default since it had a green table cloth and was also the only table that still had empty seats. The two ladies already seated next to one another, one with red hair, the other with gray, eyed Lily's fuzzy dice with envy.

"Hello," I said to them. "We're both new to the game, so apologies ahead of time if we aren't very good." I took the seat opposite the woman with red hair. "Looks like you're my new partner, right?"

Red Hair nodded. "That's right. You'll switch partners each round."

"Got it. Sorry again for all the questions. This is our

first time playing."

"Oh," said Gray Hair, "that's no trouble." She gave the green dice a covetous glance. "It's more a game of luck than anything else."

Lily's eyes narrowed, and she clutched the oversized dice tighter, stroking it with an impeccably manicured hand. "We'll see about that. Twos, was it?"

The bell sounded and we were off. Gray Hair rolled a few points, and I scored zip before the dice moved to my sister.

Lily wasted no time now, snatching up the dice with her dominant hand. The fuzzy dice lay nestled in the crook of her other arm. Her roll was short and aggressive, the dice tumbling across the table with a mighty clatter. Two, Two, Five.

As Lily kept her turn going, a momentary snip of chatter caught my ear from a table nearby.

"…one of those band fellows covered in grease. And I'm sure he wasn't getting his car fixed, either. Mr. Hardy is such a nice man, too. I'm sure he would let these musicians run roughshod over his entire shop if they wanted to."

"But which of them was it?" came another voice from the table.

"Well, I certainly have no idea, Barbara. They've all got that long stringy rocker hair. Like they haven't showered in a month. Absolutely disgraceful, if you ask me."

"Poppy!"

My attention jerked back to my own table.

Lily stared daggers. "It's your turn." She pointed one of those manicured fingers at the three dice in front of me. "You're wasting time."

Grabbing the dice, I rolled under Lily's judgmental gaze. She frowned when I roll a two then another set of twos before scratching out.

When I leaned my ear back toward the other table, whatever previous conversation about Marty Hardy's shop was over and the women's discussion had moved on to gossip about Barbara's hairdresser's cousin's husband. My imagination tried to come up with a reasonable explanation why one of the band would be in Marty's shop, let alone all greased up. Boredom maybe? Nothing made sense.

The bell sounded the end to the round. As winners, Lily and Gray Hair moved up a table, while I stayed back with Red Hair. The evening wore on, and I took every opportunity to eavesdrop on table conversations, but I heard nothing more about the stringy-haired rocker.

The twelfth round ended with me back at C3 in the dark corner with Harper, while Angie was at the middle table. Lily sat at the head green table. She'd lost her fuzzy dice sometime during the third round and now scowled at a pleasant looking middle-aged woman with a cheery smile who sat next to Angie. The woman's hand resting on the bright green dice.

"Twelve fat L's." Harper slapped her scorecard on the table with a smack. "We've got a twenty-minute break and I need some coffee to drown my sorrow."

"Coffee sounds great. I'll join you."

We zigzagged through the crowd to the refreshments table, found the coffee—thankfully not decaf—and loitered near the snack table, grabbing handfuls of potato chips between gulps. A hefty bowl of homemade bean dip was particularly delicious, and I was happy to see that only crumbs remained of Angie's sourdough samples.

"That doesn't help," Angie said as she joined us. "How am I supposed to tell which is the best if they all get eaten at the same rate?"

"Why does it matter? Why don't you just make and sell all three?"

Angie looked at me perplexed. "I never thought of that."

"I didn't take the three of you for gamblers."

I turned to the familiar voice at the same time Harper's head whipped around, cheeks puffed full of potato chips. Charlie, owner of the Treasures of the Coast gift shop, had appeared beside us. Waves of silky chestnut hair fell at her shoulders and she wore a beautiful, friendly smile on her full lips.

"Oh, I don't know." Angie chuckled. "Dice is hardly gambling."

Harper chewed furiously and held a hand to her mouth to keep the potato chips in. "Where'd you come from?" A few crumbs escaped and fell to the floor.

Charlie shot a thumb over her shoulder. "Yellow. B3. I've got twelve losses. Can you believe that?"

Harper's eyes bulged. "No kidding? Me too. I thought I was the only loser here."

A smirk touch the corner of Charlie's mouth, showing off the dimple in her left cheek.

Harper's eyes bulged again. "Er, what I meant was… Uh, I didn't mean you were a loser."

Charlie held up a hand. "Don't worry about it. I think there's a prize for the most losses anyway, so that means you're my competition." She bumped a fist into Harper's shoulder and wagged her finger in a joking manner. "I've got my eye on you."

Harper let out a single, nervous laugh.

A bell sounded the end of intermission, and Harper and I trudged back to our table, Angie to hers, and Charlie to the far side of the room. Lily never left her seat at C1.

***

The final bell rang, and I searched for Harper through the crowd. Poor thing had crumpled in on herself with each compounding loss. But when I finally found her at table C3, unsurprisingly, she was craning her long neck over the crowd, searching for someone. I followed her gaze and spotted Charlie, smiling and laughing along with the women at her table. Charlie must have gotten a win after all.

After our scorecards had been collected, I eased through the crowd of chattering ladies and reached Harper. "Sorry about all the losses."

"Huh?" She spun around with a start. "Oh, yeah, lame. Whatever." Her eyes returned to the far side of the room.

"Looking for someone?" My voice held a hint of a tease. "A certain beautiful shop owner, perhaps?"

Harper stopped staring and brought her head down. "Is it that obvious?"

"Painfully so."

She dropped into her chair and I took a seat as well. Angie bobbed over, clapping her hands silently together. "Wasn't that fun?"

"Oodles of fun, Angie," Harper said. "Was Charlie right that there's a prize for the most losses? Because I'm pretty sure that'd be my only win tonight."

"There'll be prizes, I'm sure, and Lily has the green dice again, so she'll definitely get something."

My sister remained seated at the head green table. Clutched under a lacquered claw in her lap was the gigantic fuzzy dice. A satisfied smile spread across her face as she caught my eye, and she gave the dice a strangling squeeze.

"At least Lily will be in a good mood. She loves winning."

Angie nodded. "She'll probably get prize money. She got quite a few buncos tonight."

"She won't care about the prize money," I said. "She just wants the win."

A few minutes later, Moira stepped up to the front of the room and tapped the microphone twice to test the sound. "Okay, everyone, thank you all for powering through. We've tallied the results and have our prizes to give out. Pledges will be handled separately after conclusion of the main event."

I leaned down to whisper at Angie's shoulder. "What's a pledge?"

She shrugged.

Moira held up a sheet of paper, tromboned it twice before rustling a pair of tortoiseshell reading glasses from her pocket. "First up is our Lucky Loser. The contestant with the most losses receives a twenty-dollar prize. And the winner is…" Moira scanned the paper and raised an eyebrow. "Astonishingly, we have someone with twenty-four losses. Goodness gracious. I don't know that I've *ever* seen that before." Moira chortled and a wave of chuckles flowed through the crowd.

Harper grumbled from the corner.

"Would Harper Tillman come up and receive her prize?"

As she passed me, Harper muttered, "This is not worth twenty bucks." She reached Moira, stuffed the twenty-dollar bill into her pocket, then quickly waved away the room's apologetic laughter before returning to the safety of our dark corner table.

We clapped our way through the rest of the prizes, celebrating each achievement with a round of applause and half-interested smiles. As Moira prepared to announce the grand prize, the buzz in the room picked up. The award would go to the person with the most buncos, and I knew Lily had to be in the running. I couldn't keep track of the other groups buncos *and* continue my own dice rolling *and* eavesdrop on everyone's conversations. There's only so much one person could do.

Moira waved a slip of paper and the room went silent. "Here it is, everyone. The grand prize. Remember, the winner of the most buncos will receive five hundred dollars and, of course, take home their fuzzy dice."

Light chuckles followed all around, but Lily's eyes were locked on Moira.

Moira straightened her glasses and glanced at the paper. "And the winner is… Lily Lewis. Team green." She clapped and the rest of the room followed suit.

Lily's steel gaze had turned to silk at the mention of her name. A broad smile stretched across her face as she stepped to the front to receive her accolades. She accepted her prize graciously, nodding and smiling to the crowd as if they were adoring admirers of her designer hats instead of bunco competitors at a small-town library event.

"I can't believe Lily won," Angie said between

exuberant claps. "How exciting!"

Harper golf-clapped from the corner. "Thrilling."

"At least she won't complain about how we dragged her here." In truth, I hadn't seen Lily this interested in anything since she'd arrived at my doorstep. And while I watched her from my spot in the back of the room, I realized that for once, I was thankful she was happy. Did I have Greta to thank for that? My eyes scanned the crowded room for the tiny old woman. She'd really put something together here. And as she scurried about her bunco tasks, I realized something else. I was really and truly proud of her.

Nine

THE DRUM BEAT repeated through my head, ad nauseam, as the band rocked out in the basement the following day. Their new music was coming along well, but the drums still clanged at top decibel with each stroke of Dee's drumstick. The only brightness among the racket of it all was Hips' melodious voice carrying through the house on angel wings.

On the second floor, Greta and I changed the sheets and fluffed the pillows in each room. This had become the routine. When the band went to the basement, we went upstairs.

Greta shook a pillow between her hands and the tambourine tucked at her side rattled along with it. "Nice to have musical accompaniment to this drudgery."

I unfurled a sheet with a snap. "It's not drudgery. You're just tired. And it's your own fault for staying up so late. You didn't get home until after midnight."

Greta grunted, but there was no conviction behind it.

As my sheet billowed and landed on the bed, Mayor

Dewey jumped on it and curled into a cozy orange ball.

"You're not helping." I gently picked him up and placed him on one of the side chairs, then returned to making the bed. "Hips' voice is so much nicer compared to Tango's. Can you imagine what it would have been like having him caterwaul all day?"

"Well, he's dead, so no." Greta tossed the fluffed pillow onto the bed and gave it a finishing chop down the center with the side of her palm. Mayor Dewey promptly jumped onto the bed and kneaded at the soft pillow.

"I didn't mean... I meant... Oh, never mind." I grabbed the cat and placed him onto the chair again.

"Been nice having them and their music around." Greta cleared her throat with a mighty hack. "To ease the drudgery, that's all I'm saying."

"Does that include Dutch?" I raised an eyebrow and smirked. "He asked about you again yesterday."

Greta scoffed and roughed up another bed pillow. "I'm way out of his league."

"But he's in a famous band now." My smirk broadened.

"Don't be a ninny. You know that flim-flam doesn't impress me."

Teasing Greta was always fun, but I let the matter drop, guessing from her tone that Dutch was not a topic she wanted to discuss. "You and Moira hosted quite an event last night. A big success in my estimation. I'd never imagine Lily could be so happy over a set of fuzzy dice."

"Erm, yes," Greta mumbled. "Went well."

"Will you do another fundraiser? I'm sure the library could use it, and we all had fun. Well, except Harper, but she'll get over it."

Greta motioned at the scented spray bottle that hung from my hip. "Gimme."

I tossed the bottle her way, and it landed safely on the bed. She snatched it up and gave the fluffed pillows a spritz.

"Why are you being evasive?" I asked.

"I'm not evasive. All your chattering is drowning out the music."

Ugh. Greta was so difficult sometimes. It wouldn't do to keep talking, since she'd only complain. Small talk wasn't her strength, anyway.

Without conversation, I carried on straightening up the room. Leaning against a chair was a guitar, strings loose and wild. This must be the room shared by Wings and Hips. I didn't touch the guitar, afraid I would break it with my complete lack of knowledge of the anatomy of musical instruments. I made a wide berth instead and picked up a duffle bag left on the floor.

As I lifted the bag, a heavy-duty glove fell from the side pocket. It was a shocking lime green, not a color I would associate with either of the guys lodging in this room. The green material was thick and rubbery, clearly not a cozy glove meant to protect against cold weather or a punk rocker's leather glove. This was something else. The glove would have fit the wearer tight, and a hook and loop fastener allowed for adjustment at the wrist. Smudges of grime dulled the bright green, so it had clearly been used at some point.

Mayor Dewey pounced and chomped on the glove, whipping it around like a mouse. "I think it's dead, Dewey. Let go." I traded the glove for a scratch behind the ears and pulled it out of his mouth. A sniff made me woozy—noxious chemicals and the eye-watering stink of rubber.

"What've you got there?" Greta asked.

I dropped my hands, hiding the glove behind my back.

"Not snooping into the guests' belongings, are you?"

I frowned, remembering the innumerable times I'd told Greta not to snoop herself. I brought my hands around to show her the glove. "Mayor Dewey found it."

"Mm-hmm." Greta twirled a duster around a lamp in the corner. "Sure."

"It's strange, though. It's like a rubbery gardening glove, but thicker."

Greta placed her hands on her hips and stuck her chin out in the air. "Is it any of your business?" Her high-pitched voice mocked the many times I'd asked the exact thing of her.

"Just look at it, though." I held the glove forward. "Does this look normal to you?"

"You're asking me about normal? Besides, you told me I couldn't forage through the guests' bags."

"I wasn't *foraging*. This fell out, and now I'm investigating."

Greta seemed unconvinced, then stepped forward to get a close look at the glove. "They all wear strange clothes. Maybe it's part of their rock 'n' roller outfits? Whose bag is it?"

I glanced back at the black duffel. It was plain, no other ornamentation or identifying marks. "I'm not sure—Wings or Hips. We should find out what it's for. This must have some importance."

"Well, you can't just take it. Remember that time

with the wax fruit? You told me to put it back, and that I wasn't allowed to take things from guests' bags. Then you wondered why they'd have wax fruit, and I said, 'It's probably to feed their wax monkey.' And then you told me to put that back, too, and said we'd never speak about it again."

I rubbed at my temples. "I'm not going to take it. Maybe a photo." I pulled my phone out and snapped a picture. Oddities were not something I would let slip by unnoticed. And definitely not without a little investigating. "Let's finish up. I want to pop over to the hardware store and ask Trevor about these gloves."

"I've been done, just waiting on you to finish your snooping."

We finished cleaning the room and wheeled the hamper and cleaning supplies onto the landing and tucked them into a side closet. The drumming had finally stopped, indicating the band's practice was done for the morning, and I sighed in relief.

I was about to take the first step when a pair of whispering voices on the stairwell stopped me. Greta clutched her tambourine to stop its ringing and hunched beside me, listening.

"It's hard to have these conversations and keep it all together." Cherry's voice was easy to make out. She sounded distressed.

"I know," said the other voice soothingly, which I recognized as Dee.

"I can't keep doing this. I wish they'd just give me the money."

"I know," Dee repeated.

Tpppfft!

"What was that?" Cherry asked.

"I don't know," Dee said. "We shouldn't be talking here. C'mon, let's join the others."

I glared at Greta.

She shrugged. "I'm an old lady. My farts fly free."

***

Trevor French and Marty Hardy guffawed at an unheard joke as I entered the hardware store. Their shops were a few doors down from one another, and throughout the day it wasn't unheard of for Marty to slip over to the hardware store or for Trevor to take the short walk to Marty's mechanic shop. Today, it seemed, was Trevor's turn to host their daily powwow.

"Afternoon fellas."

Marty tipped his oily red ball cap.

Trevor leaned over the counter to get a look at me. The metal fasteners of his denim overalls scraped along the edge. "Hello there, Poppy. Shouldn't you be getting Ryan ready for that pageant?" He and Marty both let out another hearty laugh.

"I can't believe he said yes to that." Marty wiped a tear from his eye as his laughter faded.

"Laugh all you want, boys. Ryan's going to mop the floor with the competition."

Trevor patted his belly with two big hands. "Don't be so sure. Shelby's been in here with Nick. And I know how you ladies like Nick."

"Nick doesn't scare me." Nick *terrified* me. Golden locks, chiseled body, and a gentle if somewhat dim-witted disposition. He had everything going for him. Beating him would be nearly impossible, even if I paraded Ryan around in a kilt and had him whisper sweet Scottish nothings into the judges' ears.

"If you say so." Marty winked at Trevor and they both chuckled.

Trevor scratched at his temple. "Not sure what you ladies see in that young man. Every time he's in here another display gets overturned or a bunch of nails go flying. He tripped and pulled down an entire wall of irrigation supplies the other day."

"I'm not here to talk about Nick or the Mista Vista Pageant. I've got a picture I want you to look at." I pulled out my phone, opened the photo of the glove, then held it out for Trevor to inspect. "Do you know what this is?"

Trevor took a long hard look. "Looks like gloves to me."

"Yes, but what kind?"

He scratched at his balding head again. "Gosh. I'm not sure."

"Can I look?" Marty stepped closer and peered down at my phone. "Looks like a tradesman's glove."

"What about a musician?" I asked. "Would this be worn to play guitar or something?"

Marty frowned. "Too bulky. These could be used for a lot of things, but they're probably an electrician's glove. See all that rubber?"

"Yes. And it smelled awful."

"Mm-hmm. High-grade. Most of us who work on electrical systems have a pair."

"Electrical systems?"

"That's right, to protect from high-voltage mishaps." He flipped off his cap and ran a hand over his hair, then slipped the cap back on in one smooth motion. "You only go through that once, let me tell you."

Electrical systems. Like a system of guitars and amps and cords and whatever the rest of their gear was called. But who would need a glove like this and why? I stared at the photo on my phone. Could this be tied to Tango?

***

"He's probably faking it." Angie tucked a large wooden bowl against her body as she mixed, winding her arm around with deftness. "The timing is *very* suspicious."

"What happened?" I took the remaining chair in the bakery. Harper sat in the other, chin resting in her hand.

"Roy," Harper said, lolling her eyes at me. "He's come down with shingles."

"Yikes."

Angie mixed faster. "Which means no Mista Vista Pageant. Like I said, the timing is very suspicious."

I gave her a side-eye. "Can you fake shingles?"

Angie huffed and blew a strand of brown curl out of her face. "Well, maybe not. I'm just irritated that now Shelby will win."

"Whoa, whoa." Harper straightened in her chair. "What about Dewey? He's the cutest little furball in the tri-county area. Nick's got nothing on him."

"And If I can get Ryan to wear his kilt and maybe play the bagpipes while also singing a Scottish ditty then we might win. Otherwise, yeah, Nick will be tough to beat."

Angie peered around the bowl as she poured her batter into cupcake liners, giving the bowl a good scrape with a wooden spoon. "I'm not saying you're both doomed, but Nick is, well, Nick."

Harper held up her thin hands and scoffed. "I think you seriously underestimate the power of Mayor Dewey's ginger fluff."

"He was practicing his catwalk all over my duvets this morning. That's why I'm here, actually."

"I can't make him stop strutting on your sheets, Poppy. He's his own man."

"No," I said, "it's about what he found. There was a weird glove in one of the rooms. Marty Hardy says it's an electrician's glove." I showed them both the picture on my phone. "Doesn't that seem strange? Why would a musician need an electrician's glove?"

"You think it has something to do with that poor man's electrocution?"

"Maybe. It's too weird to discount."

"What about that roadie guy?" Harper asked. "He sets everything up. Maybe it's his protective gear. He'd be my number one suspect."

I shook my head. "It wasn't in his room. It was the room split between Wings, the guitarist, and Hips, the new singer."

"New singer." Harper repeated the words slowly. "Now there's a motive."

"I also saw Hips picking up pills for pain in his fingers the other day. Dutch says Hips has arthritis and none of the band know about it. He's been keeping it a secret."

Angie flexed her chubby fingers. "That's got to be really painful for a guitarist."

"Yeah, except he's not a guitarist anymore, is he?"

Angie let out a tiny gasp and Harper's eyes narrowed to slits.

"I need to talk to them each, but the band is

constantly together either practicing or hanging out at the house. And I still need to figure out what Slomo and Cabo were talking about at the community center the night before Tango died. There're so many loose threads."

"How can you get them apart?" Angie asked.

"I know," Harper said. "You pop down during practice and ask one of them if they could help you with something upstairs."

"Like what, though?"

"I dunno." Harper shrugged. "Something delicate ladies would need a man's help with."

We each went silent. I wracked my brains for any sort of task I'd need a man's help with, but couldn't come up with a single one.

Angie's brow furrowed. "I can't think of anything."

"Me neither," I said.

"Okay," Harper said. "Maybe we don't need their help with anything, but you could just ask Slomo—he's the tall one, right—to help you change a lightbulb or something."

"But you always help me change the lightbulbs. No man needed."

Harper shushed me. "Just say you lost your ladder."

I tapped my lip with a finger, mulling over Harper's plan. It might work, and it couldn't hurt to give it a shot. "I'm sure there's a bad joke in there somewhere, but changing a lightbulb may be a good idea."

***

I breezed down the basement stairs with my most desperate smile plastered on my face. Golly, that pesky lightbulb was *so* high up and could I borrow Slomo for a minute?

"Sure." Slomo laid his bass against the wall and ducked under the low-hung beams as he joined me at the foot of the stairs.

Cabo let out a frustrated sigh. "All right, everyone, take five."

The strumming of Dutch's guitar trailed up to the kitchen. Cabo shouted, "I said take five," and the strumming ceased.

I smiled weakly at Slomo. "I guess Dutch is really taking to his new role."

He grunted.

We moved through the kitchen to the foyer and up the stairs to the second-floor landing. Daylight from a multi-paned window at the far end lit the space well enough for us to see. The four mounts and their large glass bulbs were spaced evenly along the high ceiling as though marking the four points of an invisible square.

"They're just too high for me to reach, even with my stool, and I must have misplaced my ladder."

He looked above, giving them a once over, then stepped to the switch and flipped it up. The four bulbs blazed above us.

Slomo looked at me with a quizzical expression. "Works."

"Ah, yes." I smiled, but inside I squirmed. A stupid mistake, not considering that he would obviously check the bulbs. "I'm, uh, certain they are *due* to burn out. These special bulbs only last so long, you know? It's criminal how they keep you buying more and more. Quite the racket."

Slomo grunted again, but flipped the switch off and placed the stool under the first light. "Bulbs?"

Earlier, I'd rustled through the supply closet and found four matching bulbs for the landing's fixtures. I grabbed them from atop a narrow wooden credenza I used for linen storage and dug out the first bulb.

Slomo grasped it gently with the long fingers of a bassist's paw and unscrewed the existing bulb.

Remaining casual was the hardest part. Slomo, true to his name, worked slowly, and that gave me time to think. Time to come up with a plan, a tactic. Some miraculous segue from lightbulbs to secretive conversations at a future murder scene. Nothing came to mind, so when Slomo descended the stool and moved on to the second bulb, I knew I had to act or else lose the opportunity completely. "Have you been enjoying the town so far?"

With both hands at work on the bulb, Slomo eyed me over his shoulder. "Eh?"

"I asked if you've been having a good time around town."

He held out a hand. "Bulb."

I pulled another from the packet and handed it to him. "I was only wondering since a few of the residents have mentioned seeing you around. Do you know Marty Hardy?"

He looked down at me, confused. "Who?"

I hid my frown. "Never mind." I moved to the next inquiry. "What about the church pastor? Hippy guy, really friendly. He said he saw you and Cabo just the other night, out in front of the community center. Chatting or something like that."

"Yeah."

Yeesh. This guy was as stoic as a stone slab. "So, I was wondering what you guys were talking about?

Maybe none of my business, but thought maybe it about the accommodations or something."

"Accommodations?"

"Yeah." I motioned around me. "About the house. You guys had only been here for a day or so, since Pastor Basil said he saw you and Cabo the night before Tango, uh, died."

Slomo stopped twisting the bulb into its socket. It was a momentary hesitation, blink and you'd have missed it. "Band stuff." He tightened the bulb then stepped off the stool and moved it to the next spot.

I followed him to the third bulb. "Band stuff, huh? Pastor Basil said Cabo was pretty animated. Throwing his arms around."

"That's Cabo." He climbed the stool and held out a hand. "Bulb."

I handed him another bulb, and he went to work unscrewing the old one. Soon, we were on to the fourth bulb. His short answers were getting me nowhere, and we only had one more to replace.

"Odd though, isn't it? For you and Cabo to be having a heated conversation about band stuff at the community center. Right before Tango died."

In an instant, he was off the stool and facing me with a hard, cold look. "Heated?"

I instinctively squeezed the lightbulbs' cardboard packaging. In that moment, with Slomo's looming form bearing down on me, I'd wished for my own protective packaging. "He didn't…"

"Didn't what?" His words were still slow, but there was a demand behind them.

"He didn't hear anything. Pastor Basil saw you there

is all." I forced a dismissive laugh. "And I was just curious."

Slomo stepped back and sighed. "Doesn't matter now, anyway." He stepped onto the stool and quickly screwed in the last bulb.

"What doesn't matter?"

He took a giant step off the stool, landing with a thump on the floor. He looked as though he wanted to say more, but instead, he handed me the last used bulb. "All done." Taking the stairs two at a time, he was gone before I could ask anything else.

I leaned heavily against the wall. He hadn't denied being with Cabo at the community center that night. He hadn't denied that they were having a heated conversation. *Band stuff.* Could that be a cryptic reference to Tango? But it could be so many other things, too.

Ten

THE BAND'S VISTA Tavern gig was a welcome night out. Ryan and I decided to make a date of it. We rolled into the gravel parking lot outside the bar to find the place abuzz with excitement. Never before had I seen more than three or four patrons, but now the door hung open as people spilled out into the night air talking and laughing and having a good time.

"Quite the event." Ryan shut the car door behind me. "Didn't expect this, did you?"

"Not at all."

"Poppy!" Angie's smiling face rushed toward me, and her hands flailed to catch my attention. A large insulated bag swung in the crook of her arm. "I only just got here, but Harper's inside somewhere. I brought sourdough samples." She raised the bag with a grin. "I'm going to keep a close eye on them this time so I can get feedback."

"Where's Roy?"

"He's got shingles, remember? Turns out he wasn't

faking after all."

"Shingles." Ryan said. "That's horrible. I'll send something over for him."

"Thanks Ryan. You know he's too proud to ask for help." Angie rolled her eyes. "Suffer through it and cry like a baby when only I can see. But enough about Roy, let's head inside."

Ryan proffered his arm, and I looped mine into his. Always the perfect gentleman.

The noise grew considerably as we stepped through the doorway and into the cramped and crowded space. Joe was behind the counter, taking an order from a line of customers waiting to put in their own. He was sweating through his plain T-shirt, and the rag he normally used to wipe down the glass wear was slung hastily over his shoulder while both hands were busy pulling taps and taking money.

He caught my eye, and I escorted Ryan to the end of the bar. I could finally introduce my Scotsman, the man Joe had heard so much about.

Joe's eyes were bloodshot. He wiped the sweat away from his brow with a hairy forearm. "I thought you said this would be a small thing?"

"Cabo said he wanted something small. I have no idea what happened."

A man shouted from the drink order line, and Joe shouted a four-letter word right back.

"Good for business, at least." Joe bobbed his head toward Ryan. "Who's this guy?"

I nudged Ryan forward. "This is my Scotsman."

Joe's eyebrows rose, and he gave Ryan a long appraising look. "Nice to meet you. And if you ever give

Poppy any trouble, now I know what you look like."

Most men would have wet themselves at a threat from a large, hairy, leather-clad biker, but Ryan simply adjusted the rimless glasses on his nose and replied, "Likewise."

Joe grunted, then gave a slow appreciative nod.

"Okay," I said with a long breath. "Thank you both for being so protective."

"Hold on." Joe poured two drinks from the tap and set them on the bar in front of us. "On the house."

Ryan held up the pint toward Joe. "Cheers."

"Cheers," Joe replied, then returned to the snaking line of customers as Ryan and I moved closer to the staging area.

The familiar sound of the band's setup greeted us as we approached. Dutch, sweating beading at his temple, scurried around the small raised platform making space for Dee's drums and for the others to maneuver with their own instruments. He finished quickly, pushing aside the last of the tavern's extension cords into a pile at the edge. He spotted me and his eyes searched the crowd before he frowned. I suspected he was searching for Greta, but my housekeeper had plans with Moira already. With the band here tonight, I had no problem giving her the night off from the bed-and-breakfast.

The band trudged onstage and took up their instruments. Even their simple warm up was entertaining with the stops and starts of the tuning process, and the patrons crowded into the small space after obtaining their drinks of choice from Joe at the bar.

Harper sat at a round two-person table against a wall deep in conversation with Charlie, who threw her head back and laugh at something Harper had just said. I let them be and snuggled up to Ryan instead, hugging tightly to his arm. I closed my eyes and sighed contentedly.

But my bliss was short-lived. As my eyes fluttered open, Veronica Valentine's hawkish glare stared me down from across the room. Once we locked eyes, she grinned and spoke unheard words into a recorder clutched in her hand. Like a snake she didn't blink once, and I finally broke her gaze with a disapproving frown.

Cabo approached, slinking through the mass of people and sidled up to me, opposite Ryan. He had a look of concern on his face. "Why are there so many people here? You told me this place had very little traffic."

"Why are you so concerned? Isn't it good that a lot of people want to see the band?"

"They aren't ready. The songs aren't ready. We could be the laughingstock."

"Your practice sounded great this afternoon, and Hips has such a strong voice."

Cabo twisted his mouth into a scowl. "I bet this is Cherry's doing. She's always getting in my way and throwing in her two cents all the time. Probably called all the media and told them everything."

"I don't see what's so bad about having a good turnout. In fact, I have another offer for you."

Cabo pursed his lips. "What kind of offer?"

"There's a pageant coming up and the town would like the band to play."

"Pageant?" Cabo frowned. "How big? The band's very raw right now. Very raw."

"It's a small town thing."

"Hmm."

"It's a charity fundraiser."

"Is it paid?"

"My friend said a few thousand dollars. It's in a few days. Nothing big, just play a few songs and get paid, okay?"

Cabo mulled it over. He ran his eyes over the band as they set up, then nodded once. "Okay, deal."

The instrument tuning had quieted down and Hips took to the stage, weaving around Dutch and Slomo to take his place at the front. He motioned to Dee, who strummed three times before Slomo's bass line merged in, followed closely by Wings on guitar.

I recognized the song they'd started, having heard the muffled basement version over and over while servicing the rooms each afternoon. My toe tapped of its own accord and I swayed with the beat, knowing that Hips would begin singing right about…

Hips took one step forward and opened his mouth, but instead of his beautiful voice, he let out a garbled gasp as he fell forward off the stage and onto the hard concrete floor. The crowd scooted away, then rushed forward to surround him. Ryan and I pushed through, moving the gawkers aside until we reached Hips. The other band members shot to the front of the stage and stared down.

Hips lay on the floor moaning and held his wrist. Ryan took it up gently to test the singer's reaction. Hips winced with a painful intake of breath. Ryan rotated the wrist in a slow, clockwise motion. Hips didn't scream, and Ryan nodded approvingly. "Not broken."

Cabo bent down next to Ryan. "Is he okay?" He pawed at Hips, checking for injury, but was pushed away. "This place is a death trap," he muttered. "I'll have the owner's hide for this."

"My ankle, too," Hips whispered.

We'd been focused on his wrist, but now saw that his right foot was entwined in the thick extension cord Dutch had earlier moved to the edge of the stage.

Dutch let out a strangled groan.

Ryan continued to focus on Hips, propping him up into a sitting position, but careful not to tweak his already injured wrist and ankle. He gingerly checked the man's foot, rotating it just like he'd done for the wrist. Another wince, but no scream. "Do you have any of your pills?" Ryan asked.

Hips nodded. "My bag." With his good arm, he motioned to a pile of the band's belongings stacked up against the wall adjacent to the stage.

Dutch scurried over and retrieved Hips' bag, placing it next to Ryan. Ryan dug through and pulled out a small medicine bottle.

"I want you to take two of these tonight. If the ankle swells, prop it up and ice it." Ryan's last sentence was directed at me. Hips would be under my care at the Pearl, and I'd need to make sure he was comfortable.

"What a disaster." Cabo threw his hands up. "The show's over. Everyone go home!"

"Wait," Hips said, easing to his feet with Ryan's help. "We can continue, I just need to sit down."

A murmur rose from the crowd and a few sad claps followed as Hips hobbled up to the stage and onto a stool Dutch had hastily acquired from a nearby table.

"He can still sing," Dutch said as if trying to convince Cabo that nothing had happened. "It was just an accident. And he's the singer now, so he doesn't need to play guitar or anything."

Cabo hemmed and hawed, but gave in and gave them the green light to begin the show. The rest of the night went off without another mishap, and the band sounded great. It was surprising since I was privy to the drama behind the scenes. No one would have guessed that this band was one snarky comment away from total breakup.

But another thing came to mind. Was it a coincidence that both lead singers faced accidents that killed one and nearly incapacitated the other? But everyone had seen Dutch move that coil of extension cord. It had been nothing more than a terrible accident. Still, something twinged in the back of my mind, but I couldn't quite put it together.

***

My head jerked up at the sound of the front door latching closed. I must have fallen asleep at the kitchen table while waiting up for Greta to get home. A thread of drool dribbled from my lips and I wiped it away with the puffy sleeve of my robe.

In the soft light of the single side lamp, Greta swayed into the kitchen.

"You're home late."

"You're up late."

I used the edge of my sleeve to wipe a smudge of drool off the table. "It's after one in the morning. What have you been up to?"

Greta opened the pantry and rummaged through a pile of dry goods.

"Well?" I asked when she did not respond.

Her head popped out from behind the pantry door.

"Well what? I'm a grown woman." She returned to her rummaging. "Where's the cocoa? The kind with the little marshmallows."

"We're out."

She let out a grumpy huff. "Fiddlesticks."

"Have you been with Moira this whole time? I was worried something happened to you."

"Thank you for caring," she said in a rough voice, "but I'm fine."

"You can't go traipsing around in the middle of the night. Everett Goodwin and his goons could be lurking anywhere just waiting for the moment to snatch one of us out of the dark."

"We haven't heard hide nor hair of that man since he left his calling card and vague threats weeks ago."

A creak on the stairs above us caught our attention. It was the middle of the night and the house was dark and quiet, save for the hushed conversation between Greta and me. Maybe one guest had to pee. They were old men, after all, and bladder control was probably beginning to be an issue. Any second and we'd hear the familiar squeak of the bathroom door closing.

But when another creak came from the first step on the stairwell, Greta tip-toed to my side away from the doorway. The stairs would terminate in the foyer, and the opening into the kitchen would be directly in view. I clicked off the faint light before it could be noticed by whoever was descending.

One by one, the steps groaned.

I eased out of the kitchen chair, brushing off Greta's hand as she grabbed at my robe to stop me. My slippered steps were light, and I was soon peeking around the doorway into the foyer.

A tall man was already at the front door. He passed through, closing it softly behind him with a faint click, but not before I recognized Slomo's long, droopy hair.

Greta's head appeared under my armpit. "He must be going to meet that manager fellow."

"What?" My surprise meant that what should have been a whisper came out as a shout.

"I saw that manager fellow slip out while I was parking the scooter. He didn't see me. You know how I like to keep to the shadows. He may have heard me though—Moira makes a mean bean dip."

"If those two are talking in secret, I need to know what about." I moved as if to follow Slomo, but Greta placed an iron hand on my arm.

"I thought we weren't supposed to traipse about with Everett Goodwin on the loose?"

"Then you get to come with me. Leave the tambourine."

Greta's face fell. "Fine. But you owe me a marshmallow cocoa."

I put my ear against the front door to make sure Cabo and Slomo weren't nearby. All was silent. I opened the door far enough for Greta and me to slip outside. We eased along the wrap-around porch, keeping close to the walls of the house and the shadows they created. At the corner, I peered around, looking through the darkness for any sign of the two men.

Greta patted my backside. "There." She pointed toward a bench on the lawn near a stand of tall shrubs.

I squinted, trying to make out the figures in the dark. Two dark blobs sat side-by-side on the slatted wooden bench. A tiny red point of light glowed for a moment, then grew faint. I strained my ears to hear anything, but not even a muffled whisper made its way back to the porch.

The tall shrubs gave way to small bushes, but they provided enough cover that I motioned for Greta to follow me. We hunched over to make our figures smaller and I hoped Cabo and Slomo couldn't see us or the movement at this late and dark hour.

We scurried along the low shrubs, careful not to make a sound. Suddenly, headlights appeared off the highway and onto the roundabout, curving their way toward us. I pushed Greta forward toward a particularly bushy bush and we tumbled awkwardly, landing silently at its base. The sedan rolled by and left us in darkness once again. The woody shrubbery grew too thick and pushing through dry and brittle branches would have given us away for sure. At least we'd managed to get close enough to hear some of their whispering. A faint, skunky smell wafted through the air.

"...looks bad."

"Forget about it," Cabo said. "Our problem solved itself."

"Hey little guy."

My head jerked. *Huh?* I strained my eyes, trying to make out shapes in the darkness, but at this new position, the figures were even harder to make out.

Except one.

Mayor Dewey's snaking tail waved against the backdrop of the night sky. He'd hopped onto the bench's armrest and now leaned into Slomo's pets and scratches.

Go away, Dewey. They were just about to spill the beans.

Beans. I sniffed, recognizing the foul odor of Greta's farts now mingled with the funky weed from Cabo and Slomo's joint. Thankfully they were the silent kind. I didn't need Greta's gassiness giving us away.

Tpppffft!

I cursed on the inside.

"What was that?" A rustle from the bench meant Cabo had shifted our way.

I held my breath, not just from the farts, but so as not to move. I would have stared Greta into the ground, but I couldn't see her face in the darkness, so she couldn't see mine.

Tppfft.

"Heard it." Slomo rose from the bench, and Dewey dropped to the ground with a disgruntled mew.

Tppft.

Slomo waved a darkened arm in front of his face. "Smells bad."

"Probably just a skunk." Cabo stood. "Let's go. I don't need to get sprayed by some rabid stinkrat, and I don't want the others realizing we're gone, either."

Tpft.

I remained quiet as the men ambled onto the porch and quietly disappeared into the house. As soon as the door closed behind them, I whipped around and seethed at the shape next to me. "Unbelievable. You can't hold it for five minutes? Like, really squeeze it in?"

Tpt.

Defeated, I plopped on the ground beside the shrubs and let out a long breath. Mayor Dewey appeared through the dense branches and curled up beside me, rubbing his body against the fluff of my robe. His purrs and the crashing of the waves below the bluff cut the silence. Once he'd calmed me down, I asked Greta, "Did you hear what they were talking about?"

"Nothing much. Just that something solved itself."

"That's all I heard, too," I said. "And they almost caught us spying."

"It's too bad we can't get closer next time." Greta tapped her lip. "You know, if I weren't positive it would steal our brainwaves, I'd say we needed a recorder or another type of listening device. But that'd only work if they returned to the same spot."

Greta's suggestion had given me a thought. How could we get closer? The word recorder had popped the unfortunate image of Veronica Valentine into my mind, particularly that of her scheming face jabbering into a small hand-held recorder. But we'd still need to get close for anything to work, and without knowing where they'd be, that seemed impossible. If anyone came near, Cabo and Slomo would clam up. I ran my hand along Dewey's back and he raised his fuzzy butt in response. When I scratched him under the chin, the tags on his collar jingled. *Dewey.* Dewey was always around. Dewey wouldn't make them clam up. But I couldn't simply strap a recording device to his back and send him off into the wild. Maybe something more subtle, something more discreet?

A boot landed beside me with a thunk, and with a click, a bright light blinded me from above.

"Miss Lewis, what a surprise."

I held up a hand to block the light from the flashlight. "Good evening, Deputy Todd."

"Good morning, you mean." He passed the beam of

125

his flashlight from me to Greta, then back to me. "Got a complaint about some dubious characters lurking in the bushes." He clicked off the flashlight. "Turns out it's just a pair of known troublemakers."

"And the mayor, don't forget." I scratched Dewey behind the ears.

Deputy Todd grunted disdainfully.

"And it's my property, so if I want to lurk in the bushes, that's my business."

"So you say. Except I'm the one who has to crawl out of bed and trudge down here only to find you *doing your business.* Is that what I'm smelling?" He waved his free hand in front of his face.

I tucked Mayor Dewey under an arm and hauled myself off the ground. I stared the deputy down with a firm chin. So what if I was in my bathrobe, covered in shrub debris with a twig sticking out of my hair smelling like a skunk? I do as I please. "What's your wife doing out at this time of night?"

"W-what?"

"Lovie. I know it was her car that passed by earlier. She's the one who 'reported' us, isn't she?"

Deputy Todd stammered. "Doesn't matter."

"Awfully late for *bible study*. C'mon, Greta." I took the old woman's hand and turned away from the deputy. "Let's go make some cocoa."

Eleven

MID-MORNING THE FOLLOWING day, I sat with Harper in Angie's bakery enjoying my fourth cup of coffee.

Angie stood on a stool behind the counter deftly smoothing the frosting of a pink birthday cake with an offset spatula. "I'm not sure I follow. You said you want to put a recording device on Dewey?"

"He's always following my guests around. He's the perfect mole."

"I like it." Harper licked cinnamon roll frosting from her fork. "He's a sneaky guy. There's just one problem."

"What's that?"

"Dewey's never going to wear anything except his collar. I can barely get him to try on his costume for the Mista Vista cultural heritage round. He enjoys being naked."

"You got him to wear that cute little bowtie." Angie grinned. "Once."

"True, but he was bribed with a pocket full of treats. You can't attach a big recorder to his collar, anyway.

How would that even work?"

I'd given this some thought the night before. Clearly, a palm-sized recording device like Veronica's wouldn't work, but there were smaller options—mostly ones I'd seen in the movies—that might get the job done. "What about those tiny listening devices? The ones you see tapping peoples' phones? Those are small enough."

"Oh!" Angie hopped off the stool and waddled over to the café table where we sat. "You need Sneaky Pete's Spy Supply."

"Sneaky what?" I asked.

She repeated the words slowly. "Sneaky Pete's Spy Supply. It sells secret agent stuff. It's in Vista."

Harper seemed skeptical. "I thought that place was a joke shop. When I was twelve, I stole a pack of gum from there, but it turned out to be hot pepper gum. I gagged all the way home." Harper dry heaved. "I guess that's why they call them gag gifts."

"Pete only sells silly gifts to pay the bills, but his real passion is spy gear. We went to high school together, and he was always into secretive and covert stuff. During junior year history, Pete wore a pair of glasses during a test that had secret lenses on the sides so he could cheat off his neighbor without looking sideways." Angie chuckled at a memory. "Gosh, I haven't seen him in ages."

"Hang on, Poppy. Those wire-tapping devices only transmit, they don't record, right?"

"I have no idea."

Angie tutted. "You need to go see Pete. He can tell you how it all works."

"Do you think he sells what I need?"

"I'm almost certain. If it has to do with spying on

people, he'll have it."

Harper licked a finger and stabbed at the flakes of frosting left on her plate. "Then Lovie Newman must have a running tab there."

***

Sneaky Pete's Spy Supply was hidden in a blink-and-you-missed-it strip mall on the outskirts of Vista. I'd blinked the first time and drove right past before I realized my mistake and turned around, finally pulling into the nearly empty parking lot around midday.

The ubiquitous nail salon and a 24-hour laundromat flanked either side of the narrow spy shop. Overhead, a simple sign announced the store in chipped block letters. A faded promotional image of a 1940s comic book detective, complete with chiseled jaw and the stiff, wide collar of a double-breasted trench coat, filled the single front window.

A door buzzer announced my arrival, but there was no one in the front of the shop when I entered. A wall of bookshelves lined one side of the shop, and the rest held swivel displays stocked with a variety of brightly colored packaged goods. I guessed from the primary colors and funky lettering that most of these items were the gag gifts from Harper's tale of woe.

I took up one item and turned it over in my hand. Probably the last thing I needed—a fart whistle. I quickly returned it to a slot on the display. Next up was exploding candy, then fake million-dollar bills, and finally a glob of fake pre-chewed gum. I wandered to the next display and riffled through the packaging. More gag gifts.

"Welcome." A lanky man with a scraggly beard and

receding hairline had stepped through a black curtain separating the store from the no-customer zone. "Anything I can help you with?"

"Actually," I said, "there is something I need."

His left eyebrow rose. "Oh?"

"I'm looking for a listening device."

Sneaky Pete regarded me with an appraising eye. "Listening device, eh?" His eyes darted from my long black ponytail to my pink overalls.

My request had clearly piqued his interest, but my overall demeanor probably left him suspicious.

"Did I mention I'm a friend of your old classmate Angie?"

He ran a hand over the scruff of his beard. "Angie... She married to Roy Owens?"

"That's her. They run a bakery in Starry Cove."

He allowed a small laugh. "Oh yeah, I know 'em. You know, I used to cheat off Roy's work all the time in our history class. Smart guy."

I gave him a winning smile. "Yep. He married Angie, after all."

As I'd hoped, that brought Sneaky Pete's defenses down. "What's this about a listening device? What are you looking for exactly?"

"Something small. I don't want it to be seen."

He grinned. "Gimme one second." He disappeared into the back and emerged a minute later with a selection of small devices. The first he presented in the palm of his hand. It was the size of a deck of cards. He leaned in close and lowered his voice. "This is the T-8500. Voice-activated, 200-yard pickup with ten hours of rechargeable battery life. Fully remote. A real favorite of Mexico's

CNI, or so I hear." When he spotted the confusion on my face, he added, "That's their secret service."

While small, the T-8500 was still too big for Dewey's collar. "Do you have anything smaller?"

Sneaky Pete nodded and searched through the pile on the counter before pulling out a gadget I thought was a stick of gum. "The Delta X. This is a new one, only been on the public markets for a few months. It's got everything—full integration, 200 hours audio, the works. They say this was designed by ex-KGB agents before the schematics were stolen by American operatives."

"Um, impressive." Veronica's simple hand-held recorder sounded better and better by the minute. "Do you have anything about the size of a nickel? I don't need..." I nodded toward the Delta X. "I don't need the works."

"Hm." Sneaky Pete mulled over my request, then pulled a tiny silver circular device from the pile. It reminded me of a tiny hockey puck. "They just call this one The Puck. You can attach it to anything and listen up to two hundred feet away. The best thing about this little guy is you can control it with an app on your phone."

"Like a remote?"

He nodded. "Turn it on, turn it off, listen in, record. You can even track where it is in relation to your phone. All that good stuff. It's got limited range, though, so it's not good in all situations. What kind of situation are you in?"

It seemed like Sneaky Pete had heard a lot worse that what I had to share, so I told him. "I need to attach this to the collar of a cat and listen in on a secret conversation."

"Collar of a cat, huh? Masterful move. The Puck should do nicely."

"Are there instructions?"

"Oh, sure. This is a commercial product. There's a warranty and 24-hour tech support if you need it."

"Sounds great."

Sneaky Pete stepped to the register and rung me up.

The Puck would attach perfectly to the back of Mayor Dewey's tags, It was a bold plan, but Cabo and Slomo would never let their guard down in front of me. If Sneaky Pete was right, I could control the device from my phone, which was even better. But controlling Dewey might be another matter altogether.

***

Harper cradled the mayor like a baby as she sat at the café table in the bakery. He lazed in her arms, limbs limp, without a care in the world. "He might fuss. He doesn't like to be manhandled."

"I'm not going to *manhandle* him, Harper. I'm just going to stick the device on the back of his tags. He won't even notice I've done it."

She patted the side of his plump belly. "Just be gentle."

I gave her a flat-eyed stare and leaned in and attached The Puck to the underside of the round metal tag dangling from Dewey's collar. He didn't move a whisker.

Angie hovered nearby. "How does it work? Is this even legal?" Before I could answer, she added, "Wait, don't tell me. I don't want to know."

I pulled my phone from my pocket and loaded The Puck's application software. "I should be able to operate it from here. On, off, record. It can even track Dewey's movements. It works remotely so I can listen in real time

132

through my phone."

"Let's test it out. Dewey and I have to get going soon for Mista Vista prep."

Angie swatted at her apron. "Oh phooey. You all with your pageant prepping. Roy's shingles are still flaring up."

"Good, then you can support Dewey."

"Or Ryan," I added quickly.

"If you both don't drop it, I'll root for Nick."

Harper gasped in mock surprise. "You wouldn't? You'll break Dewey's heart. You wouldn't be able to live with yourself."

Angie's face softened. "Oh, you're probably right."

"All right," I said. "I'm ready to test the recorder. Harper, you hold Mayor Dewey. Angie and I will hide behind the baked goods display. On my signal, say something and we'll see if my phone picks it up."

"Gotcha."

Angie and I dipped around the counter and behind the glass display case out of sight of Harper and Dewey. We huddled low near the bear claws.

"I'm going to turn it on first," I whispered.

Angie nodded.

I tapped the button on my screen that turned the device on. A small dot appeared, indicating The Puck was about fifteen feet away from my location. A low hum emanated from the phone, and Angie and I both leaned in close to listen. Static. I turned the volume up. Static. Then the rise and fall of a faint rumble-rumble. Angie and I shared confused looks.

I turned the volume up to max. Rumble-rumble.

Angie giggled, and I looked at her, still confused.

"It's Dewey purring," she said.

I nodded, satisfied, and waved an arm over the counter—my signal to Harper.

Suddenly, my phone exploded with Harper's booming voice, tinged with a posh English accent. "G'day to you, good sir. Have you got the time?"

Fumbling for the buttons, I quickly lowered the volume.

"Yeesh," Harper said, this time much quieter through my phone. "I bet the people in Vista could hear that."

I hit the off button on the app and stood up from my hiding spot. "Sorry. I had the volume at max."

"Dewey was purring," Angie said. "It was so cute."

"That won't happen during the surveillance. I'll be inside so Cabo and Slomo won't hear anything."

Harper fiddled with Dewey's tags, judging The Puck with a newfound appreciation. "I guess it works then. When is the big stakeout going to happen?"

"Not tonight," I said. "Ryan and I have some pageant work to get done. I'm taking him to the roof of the general store where I found Dewey hiding."

Harper wiggled Dewey's paw. "Little rascal."

"I didn't even know there was a roof," Angie said. "I mean, I know there's a roof, but I didn't realize it was a hang out spot."

"Yeah. There's a whole set up. Anyway, I'm going to get takeout from the diner and Ryan and I will have a lovely private evening with no Ethan and no interruptions."

"Ooh la la. And while you are enjoying your hot date, Angie and I are hitting Buncopalooza Part Two."

"I thought you hated bunco?"

Harper waved me off. "It's just a game."

Angie giggled. "What Harper means is, Charlie will be there."

"Oh, *Charlie*." I let the shopkeeper's name drip with sensuality.

Angie and I batted our eyelashes at Harper in unison. She rolled her eyes away. "Stop."

Angie swooped in and gave Harper a hug. "I'm sure Charlie is looking forward to seeing you, too."

"Will you be defending your crown tonight?"

"Hilarious," Harper said flatly. "I plan to roll some dice and not care what happens. There will be food and drinks and—"

"Charlie." Angie covered her mouth with one hand and fell into fits of giggles. After she recovered, she said, "Lily's coming too, you know. She popped in earlier and asked to join us."

"That doesn't surprise me. She *will* want to defend her crown, even in a game of chance." I nodded toward Dewey. "As for him, I guess tomorrow would work. He can hang out with me at the house until the time is right."

"What exactly are you hoping to accomplish?" Harper asked. "We aren't any closer to figuring out what happened to Tango."

"Maybe we should leave it to the authorities?"

Harper and I shot Angie a scandalized glare.

"Sorry." Angie wiped her hands sheepishly on her apron. "It was just a suggestion."

"There're so many odd things we don't have answers for, any of which might explain Tango's death. Cabo's and Slomo's late-night rendezvous. That electrician's glove Greta and I found. Dee and Cherry are... overly familiar. And don't forget the Vista Tavern gig where Hips almost died."

"I thought that was an accident," Harper said.

"Maybe it was. And maybe it wasn't."

"But it was in front of everyone," Angie said. "He tripped on some cables, right?"

"Something smells off."

Angie spun around, mouth gaping at her bakery.

"Not here, Angie. I meant about Tango."

"Oh, right." She sighed in relief.

I leaned in and scratched behind Mayor Dewey's ears and he nuzzled deeper into Harper's arms. "I think we should see what this little guy can figure out for us tomorrow night. It could be the answer to everything."

Twelve

THE SIGN HANGING in the window was turned to the closed side, but I pushed through the door of the general store, arms loaded with overflowing bags, and slid in with a twirl. Ryan spotted me and I held up the bags in triumph. Tonight was our rooftop date, and I meant to make it special.

Ryan pointed at the stuffed totes slung on my arms. "Oy, what have you got there in your bag of tricks?"

"Takeout from Shelby's Diner and a few cozy necessities for tonight."

"Does that include wine?"

"Perhaps," I said with a wink. "When are you done here? Is Ursula still around?"

"No, she's gone home already, and I'm finishing up now." He turned and took off his white pharmacy coat and hung it on a hook nearby. Underneath, he wore his usual uniform: sensible khaki pants and a long-sleeved V-neck sweater. Deep purple this time—my favorite. "I hope I'm dressed appropriately for whatever shenanigans you have in store."

"Perfect."

He took the heaviest bag from my arms and ushered me to the door.

"Actually, our date is here."

Ryan peered around the darkened store. "Here?"

"Well, sort of." I pointed straight up with my free hand.

"To the second floor?"

I shook my head. "Higher."

"There's a higher?"

His response was exactly what I'd hoped for. A surprise was the perfect way to start the night.

I grabbed his hand. "Follow me." I led him through the dark hallway to the ladder leading to the roof.

"So, this is your plan, eh? The roof. Never been up there. Won't it be a mess?"

"That's what I thought, too, but it's actually really nice. Very private. There's a table and chairs and loungers and everything. I found Dewey sunning himself like a spoiled princeling a few days ago."

Once we'd managed the ladder, Ryan stopped and stared around in awe. The sun hung low in the sky but there was still plenty of light to make out the rooftop retreat. "I had no idea this was here."

"I know, right? Look, there's the table. Let's set everything down, then we can get started."

"I hope you mean on dinner."

I leveled a stern look at him. "You know we need to get you ready for the Mista Vista Pageant. There's so much to go over still."

He let out a heavy sigh and took my hands in his. "I

think you ladies are taking this a bit too seriously."

I pouted with my best doe eyes, hoping to soften him. "But I need every excuse to see you in your kilt."

He held back a moment, but finally gave in to my charms. "All right, but I'll need some of that wine and dinner first."

I poured two glasses, and we settled in to eat at the outdoor table, which was near the side of the building that overlooked Main Street.

After a few bites, a few sips, and a few wary peeks over the edge, I pulled out my Mista Vista agenda. "We've already gone over the cultural style category. You'll be wearing your kilt. The next category is talent."

Ryan groaned.

"Don't be a baby. You've got loads of talent. You play the bagpipes, sort of. There're a few Scottish poems you can recite. You can build a scale model of a ziggurat out of those little medicine bottles."

"I did that *one* time and only because I had to stay late waiting on Bea Trotter's prescription."

"It still counts."

Ryan crossed his arms over his purple sweater. "If we want to lean into the Scottish theme, I'd better play the bagpipes."

"While wearing the kilt?" I asked. "Only a Scottish accent, bagpipes, and a kilt can compete with Nick in a toga."

He waved me off. "Aye, in the kilt." He shook his head. "Ethan will be mortified and I'm sure I'll never live it down."

"It will be glorious. Do you think you might go shirtless? That could help with the—"

"No."

I swallowed my wine in a single gulp. "Okay, no problem. Next up is the interview. Now, this should be a piece of cake. They'll ask you a few questions and you just need to answer like your pleasant, kind, intelligent self and you should do great."

"What kind of questions exactly?"

"Pfft." I waved a hand. "You know, the usual stuff. What do you wish for if you could have anything? The correct answer is world peace, by the way. What do you do for fun? Volunteer, obviously."

"All right, I get it. Those should be easy enough. But you mentioned a parade. What is that?"

I poured myself another glass of wine and took a drink. "Right, the parade. You remember this is a charity event for the Vista County Animal Shelter?"

He nodded.

"And you like dogs, puppies. Lovable furry scamps in need of a home."

"Go on."

"So, apparently the contestants get paired with dogs and trot them around so folks can get a good look."

Ryan choked his wine and a few drops dribbled down his chin. "Trot?"

Before he could protest more, I added, "It's to show off the dogs more than the contestants. To get them adopted." I put on my saddest frown. "Poor little guys."

He wiped the wine from his face with a napkin. "You want me to prance around with a dog in front of a crowd of people?"

"If anyone can make prancing look manly, it's you."

No response.

"Think of the homeless puppies."

He tilted his head toward the dusky sky. "Argh. All right."

"Good. That covers all the categories." I tossed the agenda onto a chair and draped an arm around Ryan's neck. "Let's enjoy the rest of the evening. We can watch the sunset from here."

We stepped to the side of the building and leaned against the low wall that skirted the edge overlooking Main Street and the water beyond. The rocky surf was obscured by the bluff and the buildings on the far side of the street, but over their roofs was the vastness of the Pacific Ocean. A beam of reflective light glistened on the water in shades of orange and pink.

"Look," Ryan said, "you can make out the side of the church now that Ethan's pulled down all that ivy."

I pulled my gaze from the beauty of the ocean and squinted in the fading light at the church down the street. Ryan was right, the once-obscured stone side of the church was now nearly cleared of vines. How curious that I'd only just learned that the church, which the entire town thought was new, was in fact much older and built through the philanthropy of my secret ancestors, the Goodwins. Those cobblestones making up the siding must have been a real pain to construct back in the nineteenth century.

"It looks quite nice all cleaned up," Ryan said.

"Mm-hmm." I continued to stare at the stones. Something had caught me, but I wasn't sure what exactly. There was something curious about them. The shape, perhaps? Or the color? I sipped my wine, swishing it around in my mouth. Then it hit me. My eyes grew wide, and I swallowed. "Do you see that?"

Ryan steadied his glasses and stared at where I was pointing. "See what?"

"That pattern in the stones."

"Eh, I suppose so. Looks like a bird maybe."

"No, it looks like an X."

The "ring-ta-ting-ting" of my phone chimed from my pocket. It was Harper. My first urge was the answer and tell her what I'd discovered about the stone siding of the church, but then I caught Ryan's eye, and let the call go to voicemail. As excited as I was about my finding, it could wait, and Ryan was here now, looking sweet and sexy and perfectly wonderful in the haze of twilight and wine.

He stepped closer and placed his hand on my waist, then pulled me in tight with a gentle tug. Our eyes closed as he leaned in for a kiss. My lips were ready. I was ready.

Ring-ta-ting-ting!

Angie this time. First Harper, then Angie. Maybe something was wrong. I winced and gave Ryan an apologetic look, then answered the phone.

"Angie? What's up?"

"Poppy! You've got to get to Vista right away. There's been an... an incident. I'm not sure exactly but Harper tried to call you and I tried to call you and thankfully you answered because I don't know what to do and this whole thing has just blown up in our faces and everyone is here and it's a total madhouse just absolute chaos with the lights and the sirens and Deputy Todd said—"

"Angie," I cut in. "Slower. What are you talking about? What about Deputy Todd?"

"Oh, Poppy. It's awful. We're all in *jail*."

"Jail?" I sputtered.

Ryan stepped forward, concern on his face.

"Yes, jail. We were all at Buncopalooza and all of a sudden Deputy Todd comes through the door with his... his..."

"Thugs!" Harper's voice came through the line.

I was stunned. They must be together. "You're *both* in jail? Where? How do I—"

"We're *all* in jail, Poppy. Everyone who was at bunco. Harper, me, Lily. Greta too. They hauled her and Moira away first. It was horrible."

"Like trying to bag a wild cat," Harper said. "You should have seen it."

Angie blubbered through her tears. "Roy's going to be so disappointed that I got *arrested*! I couldn't call him. I just couldn't."

I leaned against the low brick wall, the fingers working at my temples. "I didn't know bunco was illegal."

"It's not." Harper's mock laughter came through loud and clear now. She must have taken the phone from Angie. "Your exhaustingly wacky and enterprising housekeeper has been running an illegal bunco gambling racket out of the library. Did you know this? Those 'pledges' they were offering, yeah, those were side bets. Bets on who would win, who would lose, who would win the most buncos. *And* they were selling alcohol without a permit. In the library of all places."

With each word my anger grew. I took a deep breath. "I see."

Angie's weak voice came back on the line. "We would really appreciate it if you would come get us out."

"Of course," I said. "I'll be right there. I'm leaving

now."

Ryan placed a hand on my arm. "Everything okay?"

I let that question simmer on the boiling rage I felt toward Greta. That sneaky snake. I knew she was up to something. Argh!

"From the look on your face, I'm guessing the answer is no?"

"I'm so sorry." I peered around at our dinner and our wine glasses, the beautiful sunset to the west, the thoughtful and kind man standing next to me. "Ryan, I…" I pursed my lips. "I have to go bail out my housekeeper."

Thirteen

TWENTY MINUTES LATER I pulled into the parking lot at the Vista County Jail and let out a groan when I spotted Veronica Valentine's car, its glossy *Vista View* window decal threatening the inevitable headline that was to come in tomorrow's paper.

I'd been here once before, when Angie's kind-hearted cousin faced charges in the murder of my carpenter, but this time I entered with anger boiling on my face.

The lobby buzzed with confusion as people—likely relatives of the accused—milled about the waiting room, asking jumbled questions of two officers who tried their best to placate the agitated crowd. The young officer behind the reception glass flinched as I turned my eyes on him.

"You there," I said. "I'm here to rescue a few law-abiding citizens you have stowed away in your dungeon. Angie Owens, Harper Tillman, Lily Lewis." Gnashing my teeth, I added, "and also Greta."

The officer cleared his throat. "Is there, um, a last

name for Greta?" His voice was barely a squeak and pimples still dotted his forehead and chin.

"Just Greta," I said a little too forcefully.

He gulped then henpecked at his keyboard. "Ah, okay. We do have a 'Greta Just Greta' in the system. One moment." He quickly disappeared through an opening in the back.

I expected him to return with my friends, but instead, Deputy Todd sauntered through the opening and up to the window. "Well, well, well, if it isn't Miss Lewis. Seems your housekeeper's been busy."

"I'm sure you are loving this."

He tried to hide the start of a smile underneath his mustache and leaned back on the heels of his boots. "Just doing my job, Miss Lewis. I'm sure you can appreciate that. But don't worry, we're releasing everyone on their own recognizance. Most of the charges will be dropped, but probably not for your housekeeper. She might get even *more*." His brows rose for emphasis.

"Where are my friends?"

But I didn't have to wait for his reply. Officer Pimples appeared through a locked door with Angie, Harper, and Lily. Greta followed close behind, lips twisted indignantly, as she stomped forward. Angie absolutely dripped with relief, Harper's jaw was set in stone, and Lily acted like she was in the reception hall of a five-star hotel, chin up and poised. But my focus was on the tiny old woman with her stringy gray hair and defiant frown.

"You," I seethed, eyes narrowing.

Greta huffed, crossed her arms and turned away.

Angie wrung her hands and tried to shy away from eyes of the crowd in the lobby. "Can we go home now?"

Officer Pimples appeared again with several large plastic bags dangling in his arms.

Lily quickly selected one of the bags, then reached in and pulled out a pair of sunglasses. She slipped them on in one swift movement. "Yes, let's go. This has been a trying day."

Harper snatched her bag from the officer's hands as he passed by. "This could be very bad, Poppy. Very bad. I'm an employee of the Federal government. I can't have a record."

I sighed. "Deputy Todd said most of the charges will be dropped."

Greta rummaged through the stack of bags Officer Pimples held out and perked up once she found her tambourine. "Charges dropped? That's good."

"Not for you," I shot back. "I cannot even fathom what was going on in your head. Illegal gambling? Selling liquor without a license?"

"Don't forget trespassing and unlawful use of a public building," Harper added.

"That was Moira's idea," Greta said. "It was the perfect spot."

I pointed a single finger at Greta. "You said you were running a fundraiser. You made me believe you were trying to be more social, make friends, all that…" I flung up my hands. "All that nonsense. And here I am, in Vista's finest concrete establishment, bailing you out along with my very best friends, the unwitting victims of your duplicitous deceptions."

Greta hunched up like a chastised child. "I was just going to—"

"You told me that bunco was a fundraiser. A

fundraiser! The only one you were raising funds for was yourself."

"I don't see what your aversion is to cold, hard cash."

"Cold... Hard..." My head spun.

Harper howled at Greta, eyes growing wide. "You have, at any given time, been a thief, a drug dealer, a reckless driver, a public nuisance, a stalker, and now whatever crimes Deputy Todd's minions want to throw your way." She ticked each one off on her skinny fingers.

With each of her accusations, Greta cringed. "It's just a little business that Moira and I threw together. She and I are, uh, financially inclined in a complimentary fashion."

Harper guffawed. "You mean she's on board with your schemes." She turned to me. "Can we get out of here now?"

I placed a firm hand on Greta's shoulder and guided her toward the exit. One step and a familiar blonde bob blocked our way.

"Poppy Lewis," Veronica Valentine said slyly. She eyed my companions one by one. "I see the gang's all here. What a commotion your little housekeeper has caused." Veronica grinned down at Greta.

Greta hissed and shook her tambourine in Veronica's face.

Veronica flinched but recovered quickly, glaring at the old woman. "Spicy." She turned back to me. "Anyway, I was hoping you might have a few words to share on the matter. This is one of the biggest busts ever in Vista and I'm sure it will make front page news." She practically salivated at those last three words.

"No matter, really," I responded coolly. "The deputy

said most charges will be dropped, so I guess you've got a big fat nothing to report on, Veronica."

"Still..." She tapped a red-lacquered nail to her chin, "Seems like you keep popping up in the worst places. Just unlucky, I guess."

"Just unlucky *you* keep popping up," Harper said.

Veronica shifted her attention to Harper. "Ah, Harper Tillman. I'd say it's not often you see a government employee behind bars, but that wouldn't be true, now would it? Hmm. Not sure on the Postal Service's policy on criminal records. Might make a good exposé, don't you think?"

I took a step toward the reporter and she giggled.

"My, aren't we jumpy tonight?"

I took a deep breath to calm myself down, then pushed Greta forward, nudging the reporter to the side, and rushed through the exit door and into the cool night air.

***

With Lily in the car, I'd been unable to freely discuss my observation of the church wall and its ties to Claude Goodwin's map. Instead, I'd dropped my friends off and drove Greta, Lily, and myself home in utter silence, only the occasional grumble escaping as I replayed Greta's deceit over and over in my mind.

Greta was unsurprisingly unrepentant in the wake of Bunco-gate. She couldn't seem to understand why I was so upset, and I couldn't understand how she couldn't understand. Lily, stoic as ever, said nothing as though the whole incident was already a forgotten memory.

As we stepped into the house, soft voices from the common room denoted an uneventful evening. And that's how I wanted it to stay.

Lily quickly retreated to the back suite, and I waved Greta toward the kitchen. "Guests. Tea. Now."

A faint light shone through a crack in the library door, and Cherry's quavering voice floated through. I glanced again into the common room to ensure I wasn't seen, then flattened myself against the wall and leaned in close to the opening.

"I'll have your money soon," Cherry said. "Don't worry, you'll get paid. I just need to get access to the bank accounts."

Bank accounts? What was she up to?

"I know, I know," Cherry continued after a pause. Her voice was even more unsteady. "I said I'll have it soon. Fine. Bye."

With the end of the conversation, I quickly retreated from my hiding spot and into the kitchen. But I peeked around the corner and watched as Cherry left the library, phone in hand. No one else followed. *Who had she been on the call with?*

"Are you snooping again?"

Greta's voice startled me, but I waved her off. "You of all people don't get to police me right now." I put the water on to boil. The kettle clanked as I set it down harshly on the burner. "This has already been a long night and we've still got a lot more ahead of us."

Greta's muffled voice came from deep in the pantry as she rustled around for the tea. "You can't stay mad at me forever."

"Just watch me. And don't you dare say anything to

the guests about your little stint in the slammer. I'm trying to run a respectable establishment here."

Greta snorted. "Suit yourself."

We prepared the remaining refreshments in silence, and as we turned through the swivel door with tea and crackers on a tray, my scowl transformed into a friendly smile. "Tea is ready," I said, and placed the platter onto the buffet.

From the living room, Dutch was the first to respond. "We heard about what happened. Are you all right, Greta?"

Grr. So much for my plan. I spun around to face the group with a sweet smile plastered to my face. "It was nothing. She's fine."

"Yeah, Dutch," said Dee, who sat next to Cherry in one of the cozy loveseats. "She's fine. Right Greta?"

Greta took a deep breath and cackled. "I survived the seventies, boys. This was nothing."

I wilted inside from embarrassment and held back the gurgle that rose in my throat.

Dee stared off at nothing with a twinkle of remembrance in his eyes. "The seventies, man, that was the best. Arrested maybe a dozen times. I've still got my mug shots framed back at home."

"Same," said Slomo nodding. "Maybe ten."

Hips added his two cents. "Just twice for me. I guess I was a good boy back then."

Wings strummed from an acoustic guitar on his lap. "I remember '79 like it was yesterday. Drugs, booze, girls. Friend and I stole my pop's Camaro and caused such a ruckus the sheriff chased us down one night." He slapped the side of the chair. "Poor sheriff didn't know his son was riding shotgun!"

The whole band burst out laughing and I smiled weakly, managing a tepid chuckle.

"I remember once," Dee said, "Tango and I were at some grimy local hole. We couldn't have been more than fifteen. Band was absolute trash, but we didn't care. We snuck in through the bathroom window because we didn't have cover money. Tango's belt loop got caught on the sill and ripped his jeans clean in half and they were just dangling there. He went with it, though. Strode into the place like the king of punk fashion. Man…" Dee choked up. "He was the best."

Cherry reached over and rubbed Dee on the back. He gestured silently that he was okay.

"He was a quality guy," Hips said.

Wings plucked an off-key note and everyone looked his way. He said nothing and turned his interest to tuning the guitar, but the intention wasn't lost on the group. Dee bristled and Hips frowned, shaking his head.

"Hey, Poppy." Slomo's deep voice broke the awkwardness, and I was grateful for the small favor. "You need better wire caps."

"Better what?"

"Wire caps."

"It'll take an hour to get it out of him," Wings said. "He means you need better quality caps on your electrical wires. He said your lighting was all messed up."

"What?" I barked. "I just had the house rewired last summer."

Slomo shrugged.

I turned to Wings, and he shrugged too.

Wings nodded toward Slomo. "You should listen to

him. He may be a quiet musician now, but he used to be all sorts of things. An electrician, a carpenter, a mechanic. That's how we met, working in a chop shop together. He never talked much back then, either. Those jobs were perfect, no talking needed."

Slomo nodded in a slow rhythm.

An electrician? No wonder changing my bulbs was a cinch. My immediate irritation at Cho's apparent shoddy electrical work last summer was forgotten as soon as this information was shared.

Cabo looked up from the crossword puzzle he'd been scribbling away at for two days. "Speaking of electrical, have you heard anything from that deputy of yours about the investigation?"

"No," I replied. "And you should get comfortable because from my experience, Vista County investigations move in time with glaciers."

Cabo frowned and went back to muttering over his crossword. Without looking up, he said, "They seem to be on top of everything else, based on the turnout at the Vista Tavern the other night. Wonder how so many people found out about our *secret* show?" The question faded on his lips, clearly rhetorical, meant more to insinuate than garner an actual answer. "Wish people wouldn't meddle."

Cherry stared daggers at Cabo and looked as though she were about to say something plainly when Dee spoke first. "Cool it, Cabo. No one's here to cause trouble."

"Mm-hmm," Cabo mumbled from behind the crossword.

Tensions were getting heated in this house, and I wished Deputy Todd and whatever specialists he had working on that electrical report would hurry it up.

But we didn't have to sit on our hands and wait for our bungling deputy and the county investigatory nitwit crew. I poured a cup of caffeinated black tea and gulped it down then poured another and handed it to Greta. "Drink up. We're on Dewey snoop duty tonight."

***

The Pearl was dead quiet as the clock struck midnight, and Greta, Dewey, and I sat quietly at the small kitchen table in the darkness, waiting for what we hoped would be two roving middle-aged men with a stinky joint. Dewey, like clockwork, had arrived not long after nine prowling around for some late-night pets. The Puck remained fixed on his tags and my phone was fully charged and ready to listen in on any covert confessions.

At this late hour and despite drinking two black teas, my eyes drooped, and I slumped in my chair with Dewey cradled in my lap. Greta sat upright opposite me, short legs dangling above the floor. We waited with the lights off to make sure not to let on to our spying. A silvery haze of moonlight shone through the open window above the sink and gave off just enough light to make out shapes once my eyes had grown accustomed. The dimness did not help me stay awake, though, and as soon as my eyelids jerked open, they'd start to droop once more.

"No sleeping," Greta whispered in a low, husky voice. "You pumped me full of tea and now I'm as perky as a parrot and my bladder's full to bursting."

I put a finger to my lip to shush her just as familiar creaks sounded on the stair landing on the second floor above our heads. A moment later and the front door creaked open, then shut with a faint click.

Greta hopped off her chair and then onto her stool in front of the sink. She peered out the corner of the window, then turned and with a single nod of her head, I knew Slomo and Cabo were once again on their late-night rendezvous.

Dewey purred in my lap, and loath as I was to disturb a sleeping cat, I eased him up and into my arms. He let out a groggy meow as I set him on his feet and checked to make sure The Puck remained secured.

I opened the application on my phone and turned on the device remotely. A tiny dot appeared on screen showing The Puck's location. I leaned into Dewey's warm chest fur and whispered, "Hello."

A faint echo came from my phone and I knew we were in business. I scooped the mayor up and carried him to the open window. He crawled out without prompting and landed silently on the porch.

If I knew Dewey, he might meander around, but ultimately, he'd seek the nearest warm lap, which I hoped was currently taking a seat at the bench in my yard.

Greta and I squinted through the window, keeping low so we weren't seen.

Greta's volume was equally low. "He's just washing a paw on the railing."

"Give him some time. I'm more worried the skunky smell will deter him."

"Didn't bother him the other night. Maybe he likes it."

I held my phone up to my ear. Slurp. Slurp. At least the sound was working.

"There," Greta said. "He's on the move."

Dewey had jumped off the railing and pushed up against the post, rubbed his back along the corner edge, then flicked his tail. He took the steps down to the lawn catlike and silent, and sauntered across the grass to the two figures on the bench.

"Hey cat." Slomo's voice seemed odd until I realized it was coming from my phone. It had worked!

Greta and I held the phone close to our ears. The deep rumble of Dewey's purrs drowned out Cabo's response. A sharp crackling came through the phone, and we both jerked our ears away. I peeked out the window. Slomo kept rustling Dewey's collar.

Finally, Mayor Dewey settled into Slomo's lap, and his purring, although constant, was soft enough that the two men's voices came through clearly.

"Is your cousin still interested?" Cabo asked.

"Yeah."

"Good. Good. Always good to have interest in the band's future. We may need to call on him sooner rather than later."

"Why?"

"Just because, okay? Trust me. We've got a ways to go before we're back to number one."

Slomo grunted.

"We just have to lie low," Cabo said, "then we can talk about changes."

"And Dutch?"

Cabo grumbled at the mention of the roadie. "We'll deal with him when the time comes. You have to trust me."

"Trust, huh?"

"Look, I know things didn't go according to plan, but

it turned out in the end. Tango's finally gone, just like we wanted. Now we can move forward with Hips on vocals."

I held my breath. This was close to a confession. Tango gone. Hips on vocals. What exactly was their plan? And Dutch... Was he now in danger?

Greta's brow furrowed. She must be wondering the same.

"Gimme that," Cabo said before a long, drawn-out exhale came through my phone followed by a fit of light coughing. "Just lie low. You're good at that. No one has to know."

"Poppy said something."

At mention of my name, I let out a gasp. Greta tsked her disapproval.

"What? What did she say?"

"Someone saw us."

Cabo's spoke through clenched teeth. "There has to be more than that. For once, could you use more than three words?"

Slomo's tone didn't change, still low and slow. "Said someone saw us at the community center. Your arms where flailing."

"My arms do not—never mind. Did she say anything else? Did she hear what we were talking about?"

"Don't think so."

"I'll have to keep a closer eye on her." Another slow exhale. "Come on, let's go back in. It's getting cold."

"But the cat."

"Forget the cat."

Cabo must have disturbed him because Dewey let out an annoyed meow. A few moments later the cat jumped through the window and into the kitchen with me and

Greta.

I turned off the device's application on my phone and we scrambled to the darkest corner of the kitchen. There, we waited for the door to open and close and for the creaking stairs to signal that Cabo and Slomo had returned to their rooms.

"Sounds like a conspiracy," Greta said.

"Sounded like a confession to me. Do you think they'd do something to Dutch?"

Greta shrugged. "If they could do something to that screeching banshee of a singer, they could do something to that flabby roadie."

"Maybe I should take this information to Deputy Todd. If Dutch is in danger—"

"Don't you dare," Greta snapped. "Deputy Nitwit already told you to stay out of it and they didn't confess to anything, despite what you thought you heard."

I weighed my options. "I guess you're right. And Deputy Todd would probably double down on your bunco charges."

Greta nodded and smiled smugly as though she'd convinced me to change my mind.

"But we have to do something," I said. "Now that you're not tied up with scamming Vista County residents out of their money, you can keep an eye on Dutch."

That wiped the smile right off her face.

"Make sure he's safe," I said.

Her mouth dropped open. "But I—"

"Stay close to him. *Really* close."

"I don't think—"

I crossed my arms triumphantly and mirrored Greta's smug smile from a moment ago. "This will be a great opportunity for you to earn back my trust. I'm depending on you, so don't let me down. After all, Deputy Nitwit is just a phone call away."

Fourteen

GRETA GRUMBLED THE entire walk to the bakery. "I thought you said I had to watch Dutch?"

"This is important, and I'm not ready to have you out of my sight. Plus, the other band members should keep Cabo and Slomo honest until we get back."

"Did that logic help Tango?"

I skipped a step at that, but continued on. Dutch would just have to fend for himself for a few minutes. I had to fill Harper and Angie in on the odd pattern in the church's stone wall, a detailed explanation of which Greta had already received that morning.

We pushed through the bakery door to the familiar chime and, unsurprisingly, Harper sat at the lone table, her tight brown curls were messy and her eyes nearly closed. She looked ragged. Angie, rosy-cheeked as ever, kneaded dough behind the counter with one aggressive grunt after another.

"What's she doing here?" Harper gave Greta the side-eye.

"She's on a tight leash," I said.

"Cinnamon rolls and coffee?"

"Yes, thanks Angie."

"No coffee for me." Greta dug a hand into the front of her dress and pulled out a silvery flask.

Harper rolled her eyes toward me.

"I pick my battles," I said, exasperated.

"Oh yeah? How about this battle?" She slapped a rolled-up newspaper onto the table.

I unfurled it and read the headline aloud. "Bunco Babes Busted."

Angie scurried over and placed the steaming coffee and gooey cinnamon rolls on the table. "We had to know Veronica would write something about it. Thankfully, the only names mentioned are Greta's and the librarian's, and Greta's doesn't even list a last name."

"Moira will be lucky to keep her job." I checked to see if Greta showed any reaction, remorse or guilt, but she'd already dug into the cinnamon roll and paid no attention.

Harper dipped her head at Greta. "I'm surprised this one still has hers."

"Like I said, she's on a short leash. But I'm not here about Greta's lawlessness. I want to tell you about what I found last night with Ryan."

"Ooh, Ryan." Angie cooed with delight and pulled over a stool and sat with us at the table. "On the roof?"

"No, at the church."

"I thought you were on the roof."

"Sorry," I said. "Let me back up. Ryan and I were on the roof—it went well, by the way, until I got your call about Greta." I spared another glare for Greta. "Anyway, we were taking in the sunset and the church was in that same direction. Ethan had already pulled down all that overgrown ivy from the wall for some volunteer project and lo-and-behold, there was a pattern in the stones."

"A pattern?" Harper repeated.

"Not just any pattern. It was in the shape of an X."

"Whoa," Harper said. "Is that our X-marks-the-spot?"

"Gosh," Angie whispered.

Greta licked her fork with a wriggly tongue then pointed the utensil at me. "I surmise your ancestor may have used his influence to rebuild that church for a reason."

"I think so, too," I said. "And whatever it is, he laid the crumbs for us to find that map."

"For *you* to find it," Greta said. "There's a reason that house has been passed down in your family for generations."

That bit of information had been a surprise, learning that Claude Goodwin had stipulated that his grand Victorian could only be inherited by a member of his bloodline. And I'd thought my uncle Arthur had simply stumbled upon this enormous house on accident. I had to roll my eyes at my naivety.

"We should go check it out. The best vantage point is from the general store roof. Angie, can you take a short field trip?"

Angie glanced at the opening to the back kitchen. "Cesar's working today, so I can probably slip away for a few minutes at least."

Harper eased herself up from her chair.

"Everything okay?" I asked her.

She stretched her long arms and yawned. "It's been crazy with the pageant. Do you know how tough it was to convince the county organizers that we could move the venue this close to the event date? The town is lucky they agreed to have it on Main Street instead of pulling the thing altogether." A bone cracked in her shoulder. "Oof, I've been stretched too thin." She shot a glare at Greta. "And getting arrested didn't help."

Greta took a swig from her flask. "Let's go. I've got to get back and babysit Flabbypants."

Angie looked up at me in confusion. "Who's 'Flabbypants'?"

"She means Dutch. I can't believe I almost forgot to tell you what we overheard during last night's recon."

"The Puck!" Angie said excitedly.

I quickly filled Harper and Angie in on the details of Cabo and Slomo's conversation and my fears about Dutch's safety.

"What do you think they were plotting to do?" Angie asked.

"No idea. But it couldn't have been good if they were being so covert about it."

"That Cabo guy has a lot of nerve threatening this town," Harper said. "Sounds like he's got some slimy secrets of his own."

As we left the bakery, I was left with more confusion than clarity. Cabo and Slomo could be dangerous, but they were obviously keeping a dark secret from the others. And the pattern on the church's stone wall was seared into my brain as if mocking me. I hoped that after seeing it for themselves, the others might have some insight on what to do next.

***

We set off across the street to the general store, Harper at my side, with Angie and Greta not far behind. A clanking caught my attention a few storefronts down. It was Marty Hardy's mechanic shop. "Lots of noise from Marty today."

"Cesar told me he's working on a vintage car he just got in."

"Sounds riveting," Harper said dismissively. "Lots of oil and rust and sweat."

I opened the door and let the others file into the general store before me. Ryan, cloistered in the pharmacy nook in the back, was helping Mrs. Perez. He raised an eyebrow as my troupe of misfits streamed in. I gave him a little wave and headed over. He deserved an apology for ditching him the previous night.

Mrs. Perez gathered her purse and paper prescription bag. "Thank you, Dr. MacKenzie. I hope this helps."

"Aye, it'll do the trick."

Mrs. Perez turned and flinched when she saw me, then scurried aside and left the shop.

"Hey," I said to Ryan once Mrs. Perez had gone. "What was that about?"

He held up a rolled-up copy of the *Vista View*.

"Oh." I turned and frowned once again at my housekeeper before returning to Ryan. "Sorry about last night." I gestured to the paper. "I guess you know why."

"Aye, sounds like Greta's acting out a bit. Have you thought about having her take up carpentry? It's done wonders for Ethan." A wide grin spread across his face.

I appreciated his understanding and knew that a bit

of humor meant he wasn't mad, disappointed, or upset at all. I leaned closer into the plexiglass. "MVP is coming up soon. I'm excited. Are you?"

"Eh." He straightened his glasses. "I'm excited that you're excited."

"That's good enough for me. Look, I brought the girls to show them the roof, so we'll catch up later, okay?"

I stepped away and joined the three women talking to Ursula, who seemed to be in a perpetual state of organizing and straightening up behind the general store counter. No Ethan today. *Probably why it's so clean.*

"Hi ladies," she said, sparing an extra glance for Greta, who rarely made appearances in town.

"Hey, Ursula," I said. "Can we pop up to the roof? I want to show everyone the setup."

"Sure." She waved us toward the back.

As we approached the ladder that led to the roof, Angie sputtered meek protestations.

"C'mon, Angie," Harper said. "It's just a few steps."

"My legs don't reach that high."

Greta huffed and hiked up her long skirt above her knees. "Don't be such a pansy." She took the rungs one after another, keeping her skirt out of the way of her feet and pushed the lid off the skylight to make her way onto the roof.

Harper turned to Angie. "See?"

Angie, speechless, but faced with the reality that even Greta could do it, put one foot on the bottom rung and soon she too was on the roof.

I was the last up, and when I was topside, the others had already made their way to the side of the building. It overlooked Main Street and, farther down the street, the non-denominational Fellowship of the Faith church. I could make out the figure of Pastor Basil sitting on a white marble bench in the gardens.

"This place is great," Harper said, eyeing the table, chairs, and other lounge equipment. "I can't believe Ursula's been keeping this a secret."

Angie quickly added, "I think we all just forgot."

Greta squinted and leaned against the low concrete wall at the front of the building's roofline. "My vision isn't what it used to be, but I can see the pattern in the stones on that wall."

"It's an exact match to the X from the chair map. When I was up here with Ryan, it stood out immediately, we'd just never seen it because it was hidden behind a layer of dense ivy."

"Sorry again about your date," Angie said. "Looking at it from up here I'm sure this perspective helped too. We may not even notice from street level."

Harper held up her fingers, making a frame around the church wall in the distance. "Yeah. I bet up close it looks like a bunch of blobby rocks. Nothing special."

"What do you think it means?" Angie asked. "Is his treasure hidden in that wall?"

Harper crossed her arms and leaned her backside against the low wall. "Probably sank all his cash into the rebuild and there's nothing left."

"Then why the map?" I asked.

"Oh. Right."

"It's obvious what it means," Greta said.

Harper frowned at the tiny woman. "Enlighten us then, oh great seer."

"Suit yourself." Greta cleared her throat. "Claude

Goodwin was a shrewd man. He stole—or inherited through graverobbing, if you want to look at it that way—the wealth that was buried in Gold Tooth Goodwin's crypt deep in the woods under the pirate enclave of Prosper Hollow. Claude then took his grandfather's gold and built himself a logging empire—and that big house."

"Yes, yes, we know all this." Harper whirled a finger, encouraging Greta to get on with it.

Greta shot Harper a withering gaze, but continued, "When the local church needed repair, Claude Goodwin was most likely the only resident with the means to rebuild it. Not one to miss an opportunity, he footed the bill, and the church was built in his image, with his funding, leaving the town and residents in his debt.

"Now, when you have a patron who wields that much power and influence, what do you think Claude would have wanted done when he departed his earthly life? What are churches for and what would he have exacted as his price?"

"I dunno," Harper said. "Throw a big party?"

Angie tapped a lip. "Name the building after him?"

But I knew Greta had the right of it. Claude Goodwin wouldn't have wanted a party or a building with his name splashed everywhere—he had an entire empire with his name on it already. Claude Goodwin would have wanted the church. Or, more specifically, a sacred and secure space to inter himself and his wealth, just like his grandfather. A place where no one could pilfer his grave. Unless, of course, he wanted them to. "He planned it all along," I said softly. "He designed and built himself a tomb."

As we stared at the stone wall in silence, I imagined

an impenetrable vault, inaccessible and buried deep beneath the church. It was a shout from the street that brought me out of my daze.

"I'll be back later, Marty."

I looked the other way down Main Street. In the middle of the road, Wings waved back toward Marty Hardy's shop. The noise from earlier must have been him and Marty wrenching away on some project. I recalled how Wings had mentioned his love of old cars. He must be the band member the ladies from Buncopalooza saw working with Marty. But it was his raised hand that made me gape. It was the unmistakable lime green of the electrical gloves.

***

I headed straight for the Pearl after our rooftop assessment of the church wall. The common room was empty as I entered, so the band must have descended to the basement for rehearsal. I'd have to catch Wings another time.

"Psst," came a voice from the small library off the foyer. "Poppy, over here."

"Cherry?" I eased open the library door.

"I need to show you something while the guys are downstairs."

I shut the door behind me and joined Cherry at a small table. Papers and notations were spread out across the surface along with an open laptop. "What's all this?"

"Remember how I told you Cabo was doing something funky with the band's finances? Well, after a deep dive I discovered that he's been putting it all on credit and taking loans out against the band. There's barely any money left." She ran a red-lacquered finger down a scrawl of numbers on one sheet. "And I know he person-ally owed money to my husband. I found the records stowed in Tango's things."

"That's certainly distressing." I looked closer at the final figure Cherry tapped her finger on. Not having any experience in managing a band's finances, it meant little to me. "Is that bad?"

"It's *very* bad."

"Do you think Cabo is responsible for what happened to Tango? If he owed him money—"

"Lots of money," Cherry said.

"If he owed him lots of money, maybe he wanted to get rid of the obligation…"

"And as front man, Tango was also the highest paid member of the band." Cherry shook her head. "It's too hard to consider, even for Cabo, but it doesn't look good. And what about the rest of the band? The guys will be out of work. He can't keep up this ruse forever."

This, combined with what I'd learned last night dur-ing Dewey's covert patrol made me think Cabo *had* to be up to something nefarious. Wasn't it funding he men-tioned? Something about Slomo's cousin. Was Slomo in on it, too? So many questions swirled in my head.

"You need to watch out for yourself, Poppy. Cabo may not be able to pay for our extended stay. I don't want him writing you a bad check or bouncing a credit card payment."

I pressed my lips together in thought. "Maybe I should ask Cabo for the payment now."

"I think that's a good idea. At least then you'll know."

I nodded. "Thanks Cherry. What are you going to

do?"

She shrugged. "I don't have the support otherwise I'd propose taking over the band's management. Wings hates me, of course, so that's a definite no. Hips might take my side, but he won't want to rock the boat while struggling with his arthritis and—"

"How do you know about Hips' arthritis?"

Cherry blinked at my tone. "Tango told me. Why?"

I hesitated. Dutch had asked me to respect Hips' secret, but I had to wonder, if Tango knew about Hips' diagnosis, how far would Hips go to keep him quiet? Safer to keep my suspicions close to the vest for now. "No reason, sorry. I was just surprised. What were you saying about the others?"

"The others are so used to Cabo I don't think they pay much attention either way. Dutch has wanted to be in the band forever, so he won't go against Cabo now. Dee's the only one who's really on my side."

Dee. Of course he'd be on her side, since he's been attached her side like Velcro since Tango died. I still didn't know who I could trust and Cherry and Dee were two peas in a very cozy pod recently. My hackles went up again. Cherry was sharing this information quite freely, and I remembered Cabo's warning about her schemes— the crowd at the Vista Tavern gig and the *Vista View* article. And now she's admitted to wanting to take over the band's management. "Has that reporter come and talked to you at all? The one that looks like a hawk with a blonde bob and bright red glasses?"

"No, why?"

"Hmm. Just curious."

Cherry frowned. "Look, I was just trying to warn

you about Cabo. Don't turn against me, too. I haven't spilled to the media. Not once."

I stared around at the pile of notes and Cherry's urgent face and remembered her clandestine phone calls about accessing bank accounts. Was she after the band's money? "I honestly don't know what to think."

"Fine, don't believe me." Cherry slapped down the papers she'd been holding and headed for the library door. She turned back. "Don't say I didn't warn you, Poppy" Then the door slammed behind her.

•

Fifteen

LATER THAT AFTERNOON, I placed myself strategically among the dense shrubbery along the boundary of my front yard, waiting with my garden clippers for the band to finish their practice. From what Wings had said earlier, he planned to return to Marty's shop, but not before I ambushed him with a few pointed questions.

Clad in pink overalls and an enormous floppy-brimmed hat, I pruned away at my neglected shrubs. Dewey lounged nearby on the soft grass, belly up, and I imagined the sound of my repetitive snips lulled him to into an afternoon slumber. Snip. Snip.

"Well, well, well, Miss Lewis. Lost in your hedge again?"

Ugh. Snip.

Deputy Todd and Lovie stood arm-in-arm on the sidewalk on the other side of the short fence. A smugly satisfied smile rested on his face and Lovie's bright red lipstick shone like the glossy skin of a poisoned apple. "Hello deputy. Lovie."

Lovie's eyes shifted to the top of my head and a hint of amusement touched the corner of her lips. "Interesting hat, Poppy. I can't imagine that's one of your sister's designs."

I adjusted the brim. "You're correct. She'd never design something this practical."

Lovie bristled. "I'm surprised a gust off the coast hasn't blown you away, but I guess it suits the size of your head."

"As someone who loves big hats on small heads," I glanced overtly at Deputy Todd, "you'd be the expert, I suppose."

Deputy Todd grumbled. "Watch yourself, Miss Lewis."

I knew Wings could appear at any moment, and I needed to get rid of the deputy and his wife so I could do the exact opposite of what he wanted—meddle in his investigation. "Is there something I can help you with? I'd like to get back to trimming my hedges and last time I checked, it wasn't illegal to do yardwork."

"Just keep your nose clean," Deputy Todd said. "I've got my eye on you."

"Wonderful. I'm glad to hear your focus is on protecting our community instead of harassing innocent gardeners. Bye now."

Deputy Todd and Lovie strolled on, and I returned to my shrubs, more irritated than before. I took a deep breath. It wouldn't do me any good to approached Wings wielding foot-long shears with a chip on my shoulder. Snip! Snip!

A few moments later and the door to the Pearl opened and Dee quickly descended the stairs from the porch and approached. I waited under the trellis of trailing clematis and grumbled under my breath when I spotted the look on his face. Wings could take off at any moment, and I knew I was about to get wrapped into another conversation.

Dee's voice was firm. "What did you say to Cherry earlier? She's been under a lot of stress and you've made it worse."

"Me?" I blinked, genuinely surprised.

"You accused her of undermining the band."

"I said no such thing," I replied. "I was simply asking if she'd talked to the media yet."

Dee pointed his finger in my direction. "Cherry's going through a lot. We all are, and she's trying to keep it together."

I pushed his finger aside with the closed blade of my clippers. "And you seem to be helping her quite a bit."

He recoiled. "What's that supposed to mean?"

I straightened, trying to keep my composure. "I mean you two have been awfully close since Tango died."

The finger was back. "You don't know us. Cherry and I have always been close. She needs me right now, and Tango was my best friend."

I raised one eyebrow under my floppy hat, but my jaw was firm.

"Look," he said, voice lowered to a whisper, "Cherry and I were an item once, but I broke things off a long time ago, then she found Tango."

When my jaw hadn't softened, he continued, "There's nothing going on, I swear. We need each other right now. No one else was as close with Tango as we were. No one else even liked him."

"What about Dutch?" I asked, coming up with the

first rebuttal that came to mind.

Dee shook away a brief smile. "Dutch worshiped Tango, but they were never friends. Tango kept a small circle, just me and Cherry. But like I said, we're better off as friends."

My jaw finally softened. "Well then, I'm sorry I upset her."

"Just leave her alone from now on, okay? She's got a lot on her plate." Dee turned heel and strode back to the Pearl, leaving me alone with my clippers once again. I was thankful Wings hadn't appeared for that mess.

I continued snipping away at my shrubs' imaginary overgrowth. So, Dee and Cherry were exes. That explained a lot, but also left the door open for a motive, despite his assertions. Just how much of Dee's story could I trust?

I had little time to dwell on that question because Wings had slipped outside.

Finally.

He hustled down the walkway with intent, but I stepped in front of him just before he reached the sidewalk.

He stopped short, eyeing my clippers.

"Practice over already?" I gave him a once over. "Where are you headed in such a hurry?"

He pointed down the street. "Headed to the mechanic's shop to work on a car."

"Car, huh?" I casually glanced around his person, finally spotting what I was looking for in his side pocket. "What are those?" I pointed to the gloves.

Wings pulled them out. "Gloves. I borrowed them from Slomo."

My head jerked up. "Slomo?"

"That's right. Remember I told you he used to be a mechanic? He's always carrying this stuff around and I needed some gloves."

I squinted. "But those are electrical gloves."

Wings looked confused. "They are? Then why did you ask *me* what they were?"

I waved off his question. "Never mind. I guess I'm surprised that Slomo let you borrow them. You aren't exactly friendly with the others."

Wings shifted to one hip. "Yeah, well they're no friends of mine, but Slomo's a good guy. He doesn't care much about anything."

"And you do?"

Wings shrugged, and his face remained impassive. "I go to practice and I play my part."

"But no more than that?"

"What's more? I tried doing my own thing once and Tango and Cherry tore me down."

"Cherry told me you tried a solo career."

Wings' face grew dark. "I didn't *try*. I *did*. They ruined it out of spite. Called all the radio stations and bad-mouthed me. Called every media source they could get ahold of. Total smear campaign. Cherry's good at that."

There it was again, Cherry working the media to her advantage. While Tango was a mystery to me, Cherry had shown an intense interest in keeping the band together. She'd even told me that she felt Wings' solo venture would break up the team. Just another reason to be wary of Cherry's motivations. And could Wings' animosity have stretched to murder? He was holding electrical gloves in his hands this very moment. "If you were so mad at them, why come back? Why stay in the band at all?"

Wings ran a hand through his long hair. "Man, you gotta do music, you know?" He waved a hand toward the house where the rest of the band remained. "They're all I have. I don't hate them, they're family And now with Tango gone…"

I suddenly felt intense guilt for accosting him about the gloves. He seemed genuinely sad at the loss of the band's singer. "I'm really sorry about Tango."

Wings nodded then tucked the gloves back into his pocket. "Marty's waiting."

I went back to my pretend pruning as Wings walked toward the mechanic's shop, but my mind was stuck on Slomo's gloves. Former electrician with the knowledge, tools, and opportunity. It was almost too obvious. But then again, Slomo and Cabo were definitely plotting something, so maybe I was on the right track, after all.

***

I returned inside with Dewey on my heels and tossed my floppy hat onto the hat rack at the base of the stairs. From my vantage point, Hips and Dutch sat in the common room, Dutch strumming lazily from the guitar balanced on his knee and Hips reclined, eyes closed, squeezing a stress ball in one hand and nodding along with the beat of his headphones. Greta slumped in a chair nearby, dutifully babysitting Flabbypants.

A faint cry emanated from the cracked door of the library. I took one step toward the door before I stopped. It was Cherry. And another voice, softer, mumbled unintelligible words in response to her whimper. I wanted to listen in, but Hips and Dutch would see immediately.

The answer came in the form of a furry tail whipping against my leg. Mayor Dewey glanced up at me as if begging me to take advantage of his spying capabilities. I waved him through the gap in the door with a little pat to his bum and then I quickly retreated to the kitchen.

Once seated at the small table, I opened the listening application on my phone and turned on The Puck.

"It's okay, Cherry. We'll get through this."

"I know." More sobbing. "I just need to figure out these arrangements. I've never had to do anything like this before."

"I'm here to help."

A pause. "Thanks, Dee. You've done so much already helping me with the funeral arrangements. Would you... Would you call the funeral home and confirm for Saturday? I never imagined it would be so hard to get my finances squared away without Tango. It's taken this long to hear back from the bank. Here are the details."

The Puck had gone silent except for the low hum of Dewey's purrs, so I assumed Cherry was writing down the information for Dee.

"I'll take care of this, don't worry."

The sobbing started once again. Through the blubbering, Cherry said, "I can't believe our birthday planning turned to funeral planning. It's so awful. We just wanted to surprise him."

"I know, I know," came the soothing voice of Dee. "He knows, too, wherever he is. He knows we cared."

Their conversation stopped, except for the low sobs of Cherry's mourning.

Birthday plans? Cherry and Dee were working on a

birthday surprise for Tango? That must explain why they were together so much before he died. And now, working on the funeral arrangements together. All those close and cozy conversations. They were planning the funeral. They were the closest to Tango, and I'd thought they were having a torrid affair. I shook my head sadly. Cherry was right, it was awful, and I'd been wrong all along.

With Dee and Cherry's motive turned on its head, that left me with two outstanding suspects. I turned off The Puck and swiveled through the door leading to the dining room and common room.

Dutch leaned in toward Greta and strummed at his guitar. He didn't seem to notice the stoic, unmoving expression on her face. "Has anyone ever told you that your hair is like a silver river? Eyes like pools of moonlight?" He strummed the chords of his guitar. "An effervescent beauty."

Greta grunted.

I grinned. "If by 'effervescent' you mean gassy, then you've got Greta to a T."

Dutch looked up at the sound of my voice. Hips plucked out his headphones.

Greta didn't budge, still slumped in her chair, eyes half-lidded with a displeased frown plastered across her face. "Good, you're back. Does that mean I can go?" She nudged her head toward Dutch.

"No," I said. "I still need you here."

Dutch's eyes lit up at my words and he turned to Greta. "We could play Twister."

Greta grumbled and hunkered further into her chair.

Dutch held up his finger. "Ahh, one day you'll see what I have to offer, my sweet, sweet Greta."

179

Greta retreated further behind her mess of gray hair. "Musicians…" she grumbled.

I crossed my arms in determination. I had questions that needed answering. "I'm looking for Cabo and Slomo. Anyone seen them?"

***

Hips tipped me off that Cabo may be in the basement, and so I stepped gingerly down the stairs into the darkened space. A rustling and grumbling came from the corner, and I found Cabo rummaging through a box of equipment.

"Looking for something?"

Cabo jumped at my voice. "Yes," he said, turning back to the box. "There's supposed to be a tambourine in here somewhere. We'll need it for tomorrow."

"I doubt you'll find it." *Not unless you're prepared to sift through Greta's skirts.*

Cabo flung his hands in the air. "It's got to be around here somewhere."

"Cabo, I have a request of you."

"Oh?"

"Since you've been using my basement and all."

He eyed me sideways.

"I'd like to process your payment now, if that's possible. This has been an… unexpected accommodation."

Cabo blustered. "That wasn't part of our agreement."

"Neither was this." I waved my hand at the band equipment taking over my basement space.

His mouth twisted.

I could almost see the gears working in his head trying to find a way out. "A partial payment would be fine.

Let's say, fifty percent?"

"Fifty, eh?" He sat on one of the dusty chairs and rubbed a thumb and forefinger across his chin. "I'll have to get the checkbook from my room."

"No checks," I said. "I don't take checks, remember?"

"Ah, yes." More chin rubbing. "Then there may be a slight difficulty in acquiring liquid funds at the moment."

"Liquid funds?"

"That's right. Once we get payment for your little pageant we can square up, okay?" He flapped one hand dismissively as if the conversation were over and returned to searching for the tambourine.

"Are you saying you can't pay for your stay here?"

Cabo sighed and turned back to me with a huff. "I said I could, just after the pageant."

"And what if there were no pageant?"

"That's beside the point."

I crossed my arms and stood blocking the stairway up to the kitchen. "You're broke. Cherry told me. And I know you owed Tango a tidy sum of money as well. Is that why you wanted him gone?"

"Gone? I don't know what Cherry said, but—"

"Everything she told me about you has been true, so who am I going to believe? Now, I've got Greta upstairs ready to phone the police, so I suggest you start talking." I held steady, surprised at my conviction. Plus, Cabo didn't know that Greta would never touch a phone, let alone trust in the police.

He eyed the stairs.

"No way out," I said. "Tell me everything or I'll tell the band that you've run them into the ground."

"All right, fine," he snapped. "But it's not what you think." He ground his teeth. "Cherry's always getting in the way of things. She's always had her talons in this band. First with Dee, then with Tango. You know about that?"

I nodded.

"I took a few loans from Tango, just to cover some small-ball obligations, that's all. I didn't owe him exorbitant sums like I'm sure Cherry's made it seem."

"But you can't pay your bill here. That looks pretty bad."

"You've caught me at a bad time, is all. With the pageant and another, ah, plan I have in the works, you'll get your payment, don't worry."

"Another plan? Would that have anything to do with Slomo and replacing Tango with his cousin?"

Cabo froze. "How do you know about that?"

I shifted to my other foot, arms still folded. "Let's just say a little kitty told me."

Cabo swallowed. "That's not what you think, either."

"Enlighten me."

"Okay, okay, Slomo *thought* I wanted to replace Tango with his cousin, but between you and me, his cousin screeches worse than Tango ever did."

"Wait," I said, "I don't follow. What do you mean Slomo *thought* you wanted to replace Tango?"

Cabo spread his hands. "I *may* have told Slomo I supported the move, but it was just to have some teeth to get Tango off my back. If Tango thought he'd be replaced, maybe he wouldn't be so keen on pushing me for the money, you know?"

"You threatened to kick him out of the band if he

didn't forgive your debts?"

Cabo shrugged. "He may have gotten that impression."

I wasn't impressed with his attitude. "Maybe it'd be easier to get rid of Tango altogether?"

"Altogether?" Cabo's questioning look lingered for just a moment before he realized what I'd insinuated. "No chance, no chance," he sputtered. "Tango was my moneymaker."

I raised an eyebrow.

"Not like that," Cabo continued. "Tango was the face of the band. He was the draw. He brought in all the money." Cabo scoffed. "Guys like Wings think they're enough, but they're *nothing* compared to Tango. And now I don't even have my big star. I'm in a real bind making this band work without its front man. It's a nightmare!"

Now I was confused. "So you didn't want Tango out?"

"No, the band *needed* him."

"What about your agreement with Slomo?"

"Eh…" Cabo squinted. "I haven't figured that out yet, but his cousin wants to invest, so I've got to find a place for him—we need the money. I just…" He hung his head. "With Dutch added, I just don't know where."

I sighed, overwhelmed at the whirlwind of deceit. "Maybe you could squeeze him in on tambourine."

Cabo perked up at my suggestion. "That's not a bad idea."

"What about Dutch, anyway?" I asked. "He's finally got a place in the band. Are you going to keep him?"

"I suppose we have to." Cabo let out a sigh and rolled

his eyes. "He's been scrounging for a spot in the band for years."

"He's been practicing his singing. I think this means a lot to him. It'd be a shame to let him down now."

Cabo glanced at me and frowned.

"It'd be a real shame," I repeated more firmly.

"All right, All right," Cabo said. "Just give me some time to deal with Slomo and his screechy cousin."

"Good. And don't forget what you owe me and Cherry."

"I don't owe Cherry a—"

I held up my hand and he stopped. "You owed Tango, and that means you owe Cherry."

I took Cabo's grumble as an acknowledgement of his debts, and having confirmed Cabo's financial status, it seemed I owed someone an apology.

***

Back on the ground floor, I knocked lightly on the library door.

"Come in," said Cherry.

I eased the door open and found Cherry and Dee seated in the two small leather club chairs, which were about the only furniture my tiny library could accommo-date.

"Hello," I said meekly.

Cherry wiped away a tear and Dee eyed me warily.

"I need to apologize," I said. "You were right about Cabo, Cherry. I should have listened. And I'm sorry for even suggesting you were up to something else."

"I didn't contact that reporter," Cherry said.

"Of course you didn't," Dee said, more for my sake

than hers. "And you've only ever had the band's interests at heart."

"Cabo's a scoundrel," Cherry said. "I'll make sure you're paid for our stay if he doesn't pony up."

"Thanks, and I'll make sure he starts repaying what he owes on Tango's loans."

"How will you do that?" Dee asked.

"You know how the band's getting paid to play at the Mista Vista Pageant tomorrow?"

They nodded.

"I kinda know who writes those checks. Once the other band members are paid, Cabo's portion just might be made out to Cherry McColl."

Dee and Cherry exchanged a hopeful look.

"Thanks, Poppy," Cherry said after a moment. "Take care of yourself first, though."

The redness in her eyes remained, but that glimmer of hope they'd shared made me feel better. Apologies were never easy, especially for me.

"I'm sorry for what I said to you in the garden," Dee said. "I may have been too rough."

"No," I said. "You were right. You were both right. But there is something I'd like to know."

Their heads cocked in unison.

"Dee mentioned that you two used to be together. And you've spent so much time together recently. You had to know people would suspect there was something going on."

Cherry was the first to speak. "It's not like that. Dee and I used to be together." She glanced at Dee.

"But I broke up with her," Dee said. "And she found Tango."

Cherry broke in. "At first, I did it just to annoy Dee, but then I fell in love with Tango. He was my husband, and I loved him."

"Tango's birthday was coming up, and Cherry and I were going to surprise him with a little celebration."

Tears welled in Cherry's eyes once more. "We were working together on that surprise when Tango died. Then it turned into a funeral. I couldn't do it all myself. I really needed Dee to help me."

"I don't know if you've noticed," Dee said to me, "but the others aren't exactly supportive."

"He means they don't like me."

"Which is insane," Dee said, "because Cherry's the only one who's got her eye on this band's best interest. The others are still under Cabo's spell, but if this financial thing is real, then we're in big trouble. *I'm* in big trouble."

"Well, if it makes you feel any better, I don't think Cabo had anything to do with Tango's death."

Cherry sat up. "You still don't think it was an accident?"

I waffled, unsure of how to respond. "The investigation hasn't completed, but I know what our community center can handle. Mrs. Perez's animatronic bears are no joke. Plus all the Christmas lights…" I shook my head. "I just don't see it."

Dee and Cherry exchanged another look, this one apprehensive.

"Don't worry," I said. "I've got feelers out there."

"What about your deputy?" Dee asked. "The one with the big hat?"

I did my best not to snort. "Big head, you mean. I'm sure he's on the case, but he moves slow. Like I said, I've

186

got feelers out. If Tango was murdered, I'll find out who did it."

Sixteen

THE MORNING OF the Mista Vista Pageant was a chaotic whirlwind of activity. The band prepared their gear, and Greta and I scurried around the kitchen cleaning up after breakfast had been served.

I dunked a plate into the sink's soapy water and gave it a vigorous scrub and handed it to Greta. "Are you sure you'll be okay taking care of the rooms without me?"

Standing on her small wooden stool next to me, she took the wet dish from my hands and wiped it down with a tea towel. "I know how to change sheets. It's not rocket science. Does that mean I'm finally free from my Flabby-pants shackles?"

I scrubbed the next dish harder. "You were never *shackled*. I asked you to watch over Dutch because we were concerned for his safety, but now I know that Cabo and Slomo aren't after him."

"Is that a yes, then?"

"Yes."

"Good. If I have to listen to one more story of his

adoration of Tango or his recent rise to musical fame, I might jump from the attic window."

Not that I had enjoyed watching Greta suffer, but Dutch's hopeless advances had been a welcome source of humor, at least for me. "He likes you. I think it's sweet."

Greta grunted.

"You're not interested? I heard he's in a band." I chuckled at my joke, but Greta stopped drying.

"Poppy, if I had to choose between red-hot pokers to my eyeballs and romancing Dutch, I'd choose searing blindness."

"C'mon, he's not that bad. Maybe a little awkward, but who isn't?"

A mumble was her only response, but I was only goading her, so I let it drop.

The clock on the wall struck the hour. "Oh, shoot. I have to go. Ryan's probably already waiting for me."

Greta flounced the tea towel. "Off you go."

I hung up my apron and rushed to the front door. When it opened, there was Ryan, ready to knock.

"I thought you'd forgotten," he said.

He wore a dark green V-neck sweater, similar to what he wore every day, but below that, he wore his plaid tartan kilt, green and brown with a hint of yellow striping, complete with all the hanging bits and bobs I didn't know the name for. "You look amazing," I said.

His grin was a bit crooked, and he pushed his glasses farther up his nose. "This old thing?" A cheeky twirl followed, and I lit up with delight.

"The ladies are going to *die*."

"That's not a very good outcome for a pharmacist," he quipped. "But we should get going."

I glanced down Main Street at the gathering crowd. Ryan held out a hand and I took it, and we walked down the road together toward the stage.

"Poppy!"

I searched for Harper through the crowd.

"Over here. By the stage."

Ryan and I joined Harper, who held a clipboard and was surrounded by a circle of people wearing shirts that read 'volunteer' on the back. She managed them each, sending them off one by one to whatever urgent matter needed tending.

"Oof," she said. "This is a nightmare."

"Where's Dewey?" I asked.

"Uh." She looked around. "No idea."

Ryan looked confused. "I thought this was a county event? Why are you organizing?"

Harper winced. "It was part of the renegotiated contract. When we lost the community center, I sort of had to throw in some extras to sweeten the deal. The band, this." She waved her hands wildly over herself. "Otherwise, we would have lost the contract altogether. Speaking of the band, where are they?"

"They were getting their stuff together when I left. They'll be here."

"Okay, great. I don't suppose you could scrounge around and find Dewey?"

"Harper, Poppy!"

Angie appeared beside us with Shelby, who eyed Ryan up and down with a lascivious grin.

"Nice legs," Shelby said.

"Aye," Ryan replied. "The legs of Scotsmen are mythical and wondrous. I thought everyone knew that."

"Where's Nick?" I asked. "Shouldn't you be priming him for his moment in the sun?"

Shelby straightened and said smugly, "Nick's all set, dearie, don't you worry. This will all be over soon and then you can drown your sorrows with a drink at my diner."

"You seem awfully confident about Nick," I said, "especially with Ryan's magnificent legs on full display."

Shelby chuckled. "You'll see."

"Excuse me, journalist coming through," came a voice in the crowd.

We turned to see a crack in the crowd as Veronica Valentine popped through.

"Yeesh," she said, swiping a loose blonde hair out of her face. "Who's running this mess?"

"Me," said Harper flatly.

Veronica eyed her up and down. "Should have known. Anyway, I'm here so we can get started." She glanced around. "That is, if you're ready."

Harper tapped her clipboard. "We'll start when I say. You can go wait over there." She pointed toward a desolate corner near the back of the stage. "And don't cause trouble."

"Me?" Veronica said, hand to chest as though scandalized. "You know I have an obligation to the people of this community to cover these events." She peered around again. "Warts and all."

"Is that why you pop up like a weed everywhere?" I asked. "Skulking around town like a snake, surveilling the county jail, popping up uninvited at concerts."

"Uninvited?" Veronica scoffed. "If you're suggesting I crashed that little Vista Tavern show, then you should know that I most certainly was invited. By the band's own manager, in fact. Now, I'll admit, sometimes the police scanner can be a real snore, but I have an uncanny nose for a good lead. Sometimes, you've got to find your own stories."

"Wait," I said, confused. "Did you say the band's manager invited you to that show?"

"That's right. He wanted me to cover it for the paper. He's also the one who told me about Tango McColl's death in the first place. Well, he was *anonymous* then, but I recognized his voice when he called about the Vista Tavern show." She winked and smiled smugly. "Not much gets by me. And I don't usually cover the Entertainment Section—that's left to the junior reporters—but considering the recent and gruesome death of their lead singer, I figured it was worth my time." She must have seen something change in me, because she shoved her recorder into my face and asked, "Did you want to comment?"

"No," I said weakly. I certainly did not want to comment, especially since I'm sure I'd gone pale. So, Cabo had been the one to leak Tango's death *and* the Vista Tavern gig. He'd been the one all along and he still claimed it was Cherry. I'd been prepared to write Cabo off, but now I wondered what else he could be lying about. If he could continue to lie and set Cherry up to take the blame, what else might he do?

Ryan touched my arm. "Are you okay?"

I shook out of it. "Yes, sorry. Just have a lot on my mind."

"Is this thing starting soon?" Veronica asked. "I've got a hair appointment at three."

"Poppy," Harper said. "Dewey?"

"Right. I'll find him." I turned to Ryan. "Will you be okay?"

He adjusted his kilt. "Never doubt a Scotsman."

"I'll take care of him, dearie." Shelby looped her arm around Ryan's and led him away.

"No sabotage, now, Shelby," I called as they disappeared into the crowd, then set off myself to find our misplaced mayor.

I made it to the outskirts of the gathering throng and met the band making their way to the stage. Cabo was not with them. "Hey guys, the stage is that way." I pointed behind me. "Find my friend, Harper, and she can get you squared away. Where's Cabo?"

"He's still back at the house," Hips said.

"Pardon me." Dutch squeezed through a gap carrying two guitar cases on one shoulder and a coil of cording wrapped around the other. He also carried an amplifier with this free hand. I was surprised he could still walk weighed down with so much gear.

My eyes scanned the street, looking for Mayor Dewey. I checked his usual haunts: the church's flower beds, the sunny bookstore window, and the bench outside the community center. No luck.

Then I remembered one last place he might be. Standing in the middle of Main Street, I looked up at the roof of the general store.

A few minutes later I eased open the trapdoor leading onto the roof. I stepped out onto the sunlit landing and immediately spotted Dewey, sprawled once again on his lounge chair, fuzzy tummy soaking in the sunbeams.

I stepped to his side, bathing him in shadow and he

let out a dissatisfied mew.

"You have a pageant to attend, so don't give me any sass. Now, skedaddle." I patted him on the side and he scurried to the edge of the building, onto the overhanging tree, and out of sight. I'd found him, now Harper would have to do the rest.

Stepping to the street-facing side of the roof, I caught sight of the church wall again, lit up brilliantly in the sun. There was no denying that it matched the map on the chair. If Greta was right, and Claude Goodwin's treasure-filled tomb was on the church grounds, how could we access it, if at all? *Should we?* I twisted my mouth at that last question. After all we'd gone through to figure out this crazy riddle, maybe it should be left alone after all. But that wouldn't stop Everett Goodwin's Gold Hand. I shook my head. *No, we have to find it first.*

A hoot brought my attention to the street below and I looked down upon the swirling hubbub. Harper barked orders at volunteers, and I spotted Ryan gathered with the other contestants along the side of the stage. Nick stood nearby, his golden hair shining in the sunlight. He wore a long robe draped over his broad shoulders, and I wondered if he had anything on underneath until Ryan's waving hand caught my attention and shook me out of it. I waved back, guiltily.

The band was setting up on the stage for their post-pageant show, leaving enough room in front to highlight the contestants as they would parade across. Still no sign of Cabo. Cherry was missing, too, and after recent revelations, that had me worried.

By the time I'd made it back down to street level, Harper had begun her announcements. A quick look at the stage assured me that Mayor Dewey, sagging in her arms, had made it back on time.

I pushed myself onto tip-toes and scanned the line of contestants for Ryan. There he was, lined up second from the front, ready to make me proud. He really did look dashing in his kilt—a true Scotsman. The urge to stay and watch tugged at me, but the thought of Cabo and Cherry missing at the same time was too much to overlook. I turned away and rushed back to the Pearl.

Seventeen

I EASED OPEN the front door, careful not to make any noise. Nothing appeared out of place. The library door hung open a few inches, and I peeked in. No one there. As I took one step into the common area, I dull thud sounded above my head.

Turning heel, I rushed up the stairs. I had to stop at the landing and reorient myself and gauge the thud's origin. The sound had come from the Victorian Suite, which was filled with the opulent antique furniture acquired by my ancestor, Claude Goodwin. It was also Cherry's room.

I turned the knob. Locked. Another thud came from behind the door. I fished in my pocket for my set of room keys, fumbling with them between my fingers before landing on the right one. It jangled in the mechanism for what seemed like an eternity before disengaging the lock. I threw open the door.

Time slowed as I processed the scene. The bed's duvet lay crumpled on the floor and a vase of showy flowers had been knocked to the ground, splashing water every-where. In the far corner, across the elaborately carved bed frame, Greta sat like a dingy graying doll in one of the two matching gilded armchairs. A pillowcase was stuffed in her mouth. Her arms appeared to be secured behind her back, and a black cord wrapped around her long, drab dress at the knee, locking her legs together. A muffled shout escaped when she spotted me. Her tiny feet wagged vigorously a foot above the floor. The chair leg thumped against the wooden floor after a forceful flop.

A strangled gasp escaped from my throat, coming out as a mottled gurgle and I rushed to her side, bent on one knee and working furiously to untie her binds. "What happened?" I continued untying the tight knots.

Her shrieks were left stifled by the pillowcase, but her flashing eyes left no question that Greta was spitting nails and mad as a bull.

"I'm almost done," I sputtered, but she continued to wriggle beneath my fingers.

That's when I heard another thump behind me.

Pivoting from one knee to the other, I swiveled to avoid what I feared was an attack from behind. From my crouch, I rose quickly and readied a fist, prepared to fight.

But there was no one standing there. Instead, seated low in the other matching Victorian armchair, whose back had faced me as I entered, was Cherry, equally bound as Greta was and unseen by me as I'd rushed to the old woman's side.

"What the…" But the anger and urgency in their eyes spurred me into action. I tore the pillowcase away from Greta's face.

"Don't just stand there," she said with a gasp, "untie

the rest of me. Cabo's probably halfway to Mexico by now."

"Cabo!"

Greta wiggled her hips, flopping in the heavy chair once more, trying to free herself. "Get… urmph… these… urmph… off."

Finishing with Greta, I rushed to Cherry and removed her gag, then set about removing her restraints.

"He's only been gone a few minutes, Poppy."

"I'll call Deputy Todd."

Cherry grabbed my arm with her freed hand. There was fear in her eyes. "I mean he could still be here. He ambushed me."

"Me too," Greta said. "I was just going about my business cleaning the room and the next thing I knew I'd been hog-tied." She pointed at Cherry. "He got her next." Greta's eyes grew even darker. "And he took my tambourine."

The realization that Cabo could still be in the house settled in, and my stomach sank. I pulled out my phone and dialed Deputy Todd's number.

"Deputy Newman speaking."

At first, I thought I'd dialed the wrong number, but quickly realized Deputy Todd probably doesn't go by his first name. I kept my voice low. "Deputy Todd? This is Poppy Lewis."

A faint muttering sounded through the phone. "What's the problem, Miss Lewis? I'm on duty and don't have time to jibber-jabber."

"I need you at the Pearl right now. One of my guests has tied up my housekeeper."

"Tied up your housekeeper?"

"Yes, and another guest," I whispered. "I think he could still be here. We're upstairs. If he's done this, I think he could be responsible for Tango McColl's murder."

"Now, what did I tell you about meddling in my investigation? If you think for one minute that I'm taking orders from you, think again."

"Just get down here, please!"

More muttering. "Fine. But if this is one of your wild goose chases, you'll find yourself in jail next to that housekeeper of yours." Click.

"Is he coming?" Cherry asked after I ended the call.

"I *think* he's coming, but knowing him, he'll take his time just to make me sweat."

"But Cabo could be gone by then."

"Well," I said, looking around at the three of us, "there're more of us than there are of him."

We didn't waste any time and headed out the door to the hall landing. I led the way, and Greta and Cherry followed closely behind me, untied cords still dandling from their wrists.

At the turn in the stairs to the ground floor, we peeked around the banister. No sign of Cabo. We inched down the stairs and into the common room and checked the dining room as well, but there was no sign of him. "Maybe he's gone already," I said.

"He might be in the basement," Cherry said. "A lot of the band's gear is down there. Stuff they wouldn't be using for today's show. Expensive stuff."

"Okay, we'll check there next."

Right as the words escaped my mouth, the library door squeaked open.

We took in a collective breath, waiting for Cabo to spring from the room and attack.

But instead of Cabo, Lily stepped out into the foyer. She peered around and finally spotted us. "Oh, good. There you are. I heard a bunch of noise but couldn't find anyone." She cocked her head. "Why are you all huddled up like that?"

But before I could answer, a clatter came from the kitchen.

Cherry caught my eye. "Cabo."

There were two ways into the kitchen, one through the swivel door that attached to the dining room, and another door that opened to the foyer. I knew I'd locked the outside screened door that led to the porch, and that was on a different key, so Cabo had two escape routes, and we had them both covered.

I nudged Greta and pointed at the swivel door. She nodded, then she and Cherry tip-toed across the dining room. Along the way, she snatched up an empty glass carafe off the buffet and hefted it like a weapon. As silently as possible, I crept toward Lily in the foyer.

Lily looked even more confused. "What on earth are you—"

Cabo's form stumbled through the door from the kitchen and into the foyer, arms laden with gear, nearly knocking Lily to the ground. She stumbled backward two steps and caught herself on the wooden credenza.

"Stop him!" I shouted.

Lily didn't hesitate. She seized the hammered brass umbrella stand she'd once derided, and gave it a mighty swing. Cabo took the shot to the head. On impact, a low gong reverberated throughout the house, and Cabo crumpled to the floor, out cold.

Lily appeared unfazed, still clutching the umbrella stand as she looked down at the man.

The front door swung open, and Lily raised the umbrella stand once more.

Deputy Todd strode through, spotted the umbrella stand out of the corner of his eye and flinched. "Gads!"

"Sorry." Lily set the stand back in its place and fastened a loose strand of black hair behind her ear.

His eyes traveled to the man laying prostrate on the floor and the papers and cords and other gear strewn about. Greta's tambourine lay near Cabo's head. "What in tarnation is going on here?"

I stepped forward. "This is Cabo. He tied up Cherry and Greta and was about to take off without paying his bill."

Deputy Todd leveled his gaze at me. "You called me over here for an unpaid bill?"

"Didn't you hear me? He tied up my housekeeper. He gagged her and another guest."

"And just where are these—"

Cherry and Greta pushed through the kitchen door and stepped over the band manager's form. Cherry glared at Cabo with a sneer on her face. One look at the cords dangling from their hands and Deputy Todd swallowed his unfinished words.

Cherry pointed at the band manager. "This man attacked me and tied me up. He's been embezzling from my husband's band for years and I demand that you arrest him."

"Well, now, I..." he sputtered.

I patted the deputy firmly on the shoulder. "Looks

like Deputy Todd's got this all in hand. Greta, are you okay?"

Greta stepped over Cabo's motionless arm, reached down and plucked her tambourine from the wreckage. "I am now."

The clock on the wall struck the hour. "Oh no," I said. "I need to get back to the pageant. Ryan's going to kill me if he finds out I abandoned him."

"Go," Cherry said. "We can handle this."

I headed for the door.

"Poppy."

I turned.

"Thanks," she added with a gentle smile. "For believing me."

I smiled back, glad I'd finally believed her, too.

"I'll want a statement from you, Miss Lewis. And I'll need a—" But Deputy Todd's demands were cut off as I shut the door firmly behind me.

Eighteen

A MUCH LARGER crowd greeted me as I rushed back to the pageant staging area. Gently nudging the spectators aside, I made my way toward the front, using Shelby's towering beehive as a beacon.

Angie clutched my arm when she'd realized I'd returned. "Where have you been? Ryan just finished his cultural round. He was in his whole Scottish get-up and he was so charming. I absolutely *melted* when he played *Amazing Grace* on his bagpipes."

"Oh no." I wilted inside, distraught that I'd missed Ryan's recital. "Something came up. I'll tell you later."

"What?"

"About Cabo."

Angie's eyes widened. "Cabo?"

"Everything's fine, and I think our troubles with him may be over."

Angie gave a little clap with both hands. "That's great news."

"Forget whatever you're excited about," Shelby said.

"Just wait until you see Nick recite his Greek poem. I think this one's in the bag, dearies."

Angie frowned in disapproval. "Don't listen to her, Poppy. Ryan's definitely in the running. Though, Harper had Mayor Dewey jump through a pair of hula hoops, and the crowd loved it."

"No surprise there," I said.

Shelby chuckled to herself. "You're both in for a treat, dearies. Nick's up next. Better get your sunglasses out."

"Why?" Angie asked.

But we soon found out why. The stage drapes parted and Nick Christos stepped through, draped lasciviously in a stark white toga sarong and leather sandals. A crown of laurel leaves sat atop the golden waves of his hair. He sauntered across the stage, arms flexed, and his chiseled bare chest shone like the sun. An intense sheen glinted off every tanned, rippled muscle.

Angie shielded her eyes with a hand. "What... What is that on his skin?"

Shelby straightened her apron with a grin.

I tried to protect my own eyes from the glare. "Looks like he's dripping with grease or something."

"He looks like a rotisserie chicken!"

"Looks like someone needs an oil change!"

Shelby's grin faded as snickering from the crowd ramped up.

Nick stepped to the microphone at the center of the stage. He reached to disengage it from its stand, but the metal handle slithered like a fish from his oily grasp and tumbled off the edge onto the street, breaking into two.

Another round of laughter from the crowd seemed to

unnerve Nick. He scanned the crowd, finally landing on Shelby and gave her a pleading look.

"I gotta go save him, dearies. Must have been too liberal with the fry oil." Shelby's beehive disappeared through the crowd toward the side of the stage.

"I'm disappointed we won't get to hear his poem," Angie said.

Nick shuffled away from the front of the stage, careful not to slip in puddles of oil, and peered from one side to the other looking for safety. The muscles in his back and shoulders glinted in the sun as he turned in circles.

"Hearing it wasn't the point," I said with a smile. "Seeing it was."

Harper appeared on stage and directed Nick to the side, shaking her head. At one touch, Harper grimaced and rubbed her hand on her pants, wiping off the excess fry oil. She waved for the crowd to quiet down. "Thank you, everyone. That completes the second round. Now we'll be moving on to the final round, so get ready for the Men and Mutts Parade!"

"Oh goodie." Angie grinned from ear to ear and clapped her pudgy hands. "This should be great. I can't wait to see all the dogs. And they all need homes, and it's so sweet and precious and I hope they get adopted."

"Are you crying?"

Angie wiped a tear from the corner of her eye with her apron. "I'm just excited."

A few minutes passed before the pre-recorded music began over the loudspeaker. The first contestant, whom I did not recognize, took the stairs onto the stage to loud applause, clad in a red-and-black lumberjack flannel, powerful boots, and weathered denim. Trailing behind him on a simple corded leash was a sturdy brown pit bull, mouth stretched open into a wide smile, tongue lolling to one side. The dog trotted on stocky legs to oohs and aahs of the crowd, tail blurring and butt wiggling from his rapid wagging. I couldn't help but smile at this cheerful pup who wanted nothing more than to find his forever home.

Harper's voice came over the speaker. "Meet Bruce, the sweetest pit bull in all of Vista County. He's a loveable bear who enjoys walks on the beach and chewing on his favorite stick. Bruce does well with small children and other dogs. For adoption inquiries, head to the Vista County Animal Shelter booth and reference number twenty-three. Once again, give a hand for big Bruce and his handler, Scott the Lumberjack."

The spectators clapped as Scott toured Bruce around the stage for one last looksie before descending the stairs on the opposite side.

Another spat of contestants took to the stage. There was Robert leading Willow, a faded white mop of a lapdog, who kept stopping along the stage to sniff at random bits of detritus. Robert walked her slowly, allowing her to take her time. The crowd loved her, of course. And once Willow and Robert left the stage, I noticed at least two people retreat to the animal shelter's booth.

"Next up ladies and gentlemen is Starry Cove's own Greek god, Nick Christos, leading—or should I say carrying—Mr. Biscuit, a two-year-old Chihuahua Yorkshire terrier mix."

Nick entered the stage, still draped in his toga but decidedly less shiny. Nick gave a weak smile to the crowd as the tiny dog scrambled to lick his shoulder, his hands, his face, his arm, anywhere a hint of fry oil remained on Nick's skin.

"Oh dear," Angie said. "Poor Nick. I guess Shelby couldn't get it all off."

"As you can see," Harper continued, "Mr. Biscuit loves all kinds of treats, and Nick is an absolute morsel, don't you think?"

The ladies in the audience hooted and a few high-pitched whistles screamed through the air.

"And now we have Ryan MacKenzie, Starry Cove's pharmacist and Scottish hunk escorting, uh, Daisy the dog."

Ryan took the stage in full Highland regalia, complete with high socks, fitted tweed jacket, and his blue and green MacKenzie tartan kilt. I let out a delighted giggle. He was absolutely dashing.

I'd been so enamored with Ryan that I hadn't noticed the dog that followed behind him until a collective cringe waved through the crowd. Attached to the leash was the strangest dog I'd ever seen. Daisy was dark-skinned and devoid of fur with only a few scraggly tufts of hair poking from her ears and along the ridgeline of her neck. A wisp of hair accented the tip of her crooked tail like an afterthought and her long, limp tongue drooped from between a pair of mismatched snaggleteeth. She shivered, tailed tucked between her legs, and seemed reluctant to take the stage.

"What is that?" Angie wondered in a low voice.

"Meet the pup those at the shelter fondly refer to as Daisy. No one knows exactly what Daisy is, but that's part of the fun! Her demeanor is sweet and shy and a little bit silly. If you're looking for a truly unique dog that will have all your neighbors talking, consider taking Daisy home today. Reference number fifty at the booth in the back."

"Oh, my goodness, that poor baby." Angie clutched her hands over her heart. "I hope she finds a home."

Ryan bent down and ran a gentle hand behind Daisy's ear. Her shivering lessened, and she peered up at him with watery eyes. He gave her a warm smile and patted her on the head. Her crooked tail began to wag.

Soon, Daisy and Ryan were strutting across the stage, making the most of their moment. Daisy, whatever she was, smiled out at the audience with her goofy grin and protruding tongue. The crowd soon warmed to her odd look, and by the time Harper gave them a final call to exit the stage, Ryan and Daisy had received the loudest applause by far.

More contestants and their companion pooches made their appearances until there was just one left to take the stage. After some muffled scuffling heard through the microphone, Harper emerged from the side of the stage with Mayor Dewey held firmly under her right arm and leading a spry, bright-eyed puppy on a long leash with the other. The dog pranced, circling Harper's spindly legs, nearly tripping her multiple times, and jumped and barked at Dewey, who hissed and squirmed against Harper's grasp in response. Soon, the dog spotted the crowd, and it straightened, ears perking up. Its tail wagged back and forth in a blur at the adoring faces smiling back.

"This one's got a bunch of energy," Angie said. "It'll find a home for sure."

The crowd fawned over the cute puppy's antics, clapping each time it spun in a circle and hopped on its little feet. Dewey was not so enamored and fought mightily, pushing his paws against Harper, who fought equally hard to keep him restrained.

"Our final pageant contestant is Starry Cove's mayor, Dewey, leading—Oof!" Harper grunted and tightly re-adjusted Dewey in the crook of her arm. "Leading Champ, a four-month-old—Ow!" She cursed under her breath and tucked the cat's paws into her armpit. "A four-month-old Beagle who—"

Harper's head suddenly whipped back as Champ bolted across the stage, pulling her along with him. Mayor Dewey seized his chance and with a freed orange paw, scrabbled for purchase against Harper's cheek, pulling himself out of her grasp and launched himself off the top of her head. Harper slipped backward with a thump, and Dewey darted off the stage and out of sight.

Angie and I stared after him as the crowd burst into uproarious laughter.

"Poor Dewey," Angie said.

"Poor Harper." I pointed to our friend on the stage.

Harper sat sprawled on the stage floor. A tuft of tight brown curls protruded from the skewed rainbow headband at her temple and fell into her eyes. Champ scrambled back and forth over her lap, licking her face between energetic twirls and butt wiggles.

Harper puffed and blew the tuft of hair out of her eyes. "Reference number nineteen in the back."

I pushed a path through the spectators up to the edge of the stage closest to Harper, and Angie followed in my wake. "Are you okay?"

Harper nodded, but her face read differently. I was sure the last-minute preparations coupled with managing

Dewey with an unruly puppy had taken a toll.

Champ continued to flit about until Harper got ahold of his leash and reigned him in. "We need to find Dewey. He's got to be here for the final announcement after the band finishes."

"Don't worry." I pulled out my phone. "Remember, I've got The Puck."

"Great." Harper closed her eyes and lay down on the stage with a defeated sigh. Champ immediately assailed her face with puppy licks.

***

I pulled up The Puck's tracking device and hoped Dewey hadn't run off too far. Chances were, he'd headed somewhere dark and secluded to hunker down, rather than the open air of the rooftop above the general store.

Thankfully, a red dot flashed on my screen. "Gotcha." I gauged my location in relation to the dot, turning around and scanned the area to identify his hiding spot. He hadn't gone far, and the temporary gazebos erected for the pageant would give him ample spots to hide.

I waded through the crowd, checking the dot every few seconds to make sure Dewey hadn't scampered off somewhere else. Soon, I broke away from the mass of people and entered a maze of white tents behind the stage. Some were stacked with a variety of carriers and kennels for the dogs, and others with empty boxes of scaffolding material used to erect the stage. I was getting closer.

Mayor Dewey had escaped in an agitated state, so I kept my steps quiet as I maneuvered from one temporary pavilion to another. Almost there.

Careful not to make any sound, I peeked around the final flap into the space where Dewey hid. Based on the equipment, I realized this must be the tent where the band stored their instruments and other gear. *At least Cabo hadn't been able to steal away with all this.*

I couldn't see Dewey, but the dot told me he was there, and with all the equipment, he was probably well hidden.

Two large crates sat stacked near one corner, and I tip-toed closer. My phone indicated Dewey was just behind the crates.

One more step and I peered over the edge. Dewey sat on the pavement, unfazed, and did not even bother glancing at me when I appeared. Instead, his focus was on another figure.

I couldn't believe my eyes. A man hunched in the corner, facing away from me. Unlike Dewey, the man hadn't noticed me, but I could see him. And I could see what he was doing—stripping the protective coating from a coiled span of microphone cord with a sharp pocket knife.

Before I considered the situation, I yelled, "Stop!"

The man turned, and his eyes bulged at the sight of me. Trapped between the side of the tent and the stacked crates, Dutch had nowhere to go but through me. He lunged.

I scrambled out of the way of the pointy end of the outstretched pocket knife and fell against the crates. They tumbled forward, blocking his path even more.

Dutch spun, eyes wide, and settled on the secured wall of the white tent. Arm up, he stabbed the fabric with the knife and ran a line toward the ground with a grating rip.

I stumbled to my feet and kicked the crates out of the way, but Dutch had already disappeared through the slit. I followed after, slipping through the fabric with ease but found myself sandwiched between the walls of adjacent tent structures. I looked left down the narrow corridor. Nothing. Looking right, I spied a shoe disappearing through a slit in another tent.

I shimmied through the passageway as quickly as the space would allow. *How had roly-poly Dutch made it through so quickly?*

Stepping through the opening, I found myself in a wider and more open space of an empty tent. Ahead, through the maze of the pavilion, Dutch darted toward the crowd.

"Stop him!" I shouted, but Dutch pivoted and slipped out of sight. A few spectators turned my way in confusion, but by that time Dutch had disappeared.

A few seconds later, when I got the spot where he'd turned, I followed the same route and found myself in an erected tunnel that led to steps up to the stage. From my sheltered location at the base of the stairs, I could only see a small section of the sky from the tunnel opening. I heard the crowd gasp.

Fearing the worst, I ran up the stairs to the open air of the stage. The crowd on the street below were held in rapt attention. It took me a moment to comprehend what lay before me.

Dutch lay splayed out on the floor of the stage. The pocket knife was still extended but rested a few feet away. Hips crouched over the man and the rest of The Five Foxes, who'd been setting up before their set, rushed to his side.

"Did you get him?" I asked through heaving breaths.

"Get him?" Hips looked at me quizzically. "He just ran on stage and slipped on an oil spill left by that Greek guy. He's out cold."

"Good," I said, relieved, then placed a hand at the stitch forming in my side and doubled over, bracing myself with my other hand on a knee.

Hips cocked his head. "Good?"

I held up a finger, then took two deep breaths and waited for the cramp to pass.

The band now encircled Dutch, and Wings smacked the roadie's cheek a few times to see if he'd come to. The guitarist looked up at the rest of us and shook his head. "Still out. He took a hard fall. What happened?"

I pointed at Dutch. "I caught him stripping wires on a microphone cable."

"What?" they asked in unison.

Still out of breath, I nodded my head in two big swoops for emphasis. "Chased him down and he ran up here."

Hips stared down at the roadie in shock.

"It was Dutch," I said through panting. "He's the one who killed Tango, and he was about to kill you too, Hips."

Slomo stepped forward. "Dutch?" His words came out slow and disbelieving.

I waved a hand toward the sea of tents. "Check for yourself."

Slomo took two long strides across the stage and disappeared down the side stairway.

Harper bounded onto the stage, looking at Dutch in confusion. "What's happening? Where's Dewey?"

"Stay back," I told her. "He tried to kill Hips."

Harper's eye's bulged, and she backed away.

Wings smacked Dutch's cheek again and he let out a pained moan. Dutch slowly lolled his head back and forth, regaining consciousness.

"He's coming 'round," said Dee.

Hips took a step back, putting more distance between himself and the roadie.

"Don't worry," I said to Hips. "He can't hurt you now."

Dutch's eyes fluttered open. He took in the faces of Wings and Dee, then spotted Hips and finally, me. At the recognition, he flung his arms up and tried to gain his footing, but Wings and Dee held him firmly by each shoulder to the floor of the stage.

"You're not going anywhere," Wings said.

Dutch eyes shifted back and forth from both men holding him down, and the color drained from his face.

"Why'd you do it?" I asked. "Why'd you kill Tango? We know it was you."

Dutch shook his head and mumbled a few unintelligible words.

"I caught you stripping the cords. You were going to take out Hips. Why? Why, Dutch?"

"N-no, it wasn't me. I don't know what you're talking about."

A looming figure appeared behind me.

Slomo.

Draped across a forearm was a looped length of cord, With his other hand, Slomo held open a long slice through the sheath of protective covering for all to see. He stared daggers at Dutch, but said no words. Then he tossed the cording at Dutch's feet and it landed with a thud.

Dutch licked his lips. "That's not… I don't…"

Wings shook the man's shoulder. "You'd better tell us, man. This ain't no joke."

"I… I wanted to be in the band."

Wings shook him again. "You killed Tango to get in the band? You lousy piece of—"

Dee held up a shaky hand. Wings cut off and turned away from Dutch, then launched an angry spit across the stage in place of finishing his words.

"No more lies, Dutch." Dee's voice was painfully moderated. "Out with it."

Dutch's eyes scanned the crowd, who'd been watching the spectacle in rapt attention from street level.

I followed his eyes. He'd scanned the crowd as if looking for someone. Then it hit me. "Of course," I said in a whisper, then leaned down on one knee next to the killer. "She's not here, Dutch." I said my next words slowly so they would sink in. "Greta is not here."

His face sank to his chest.

"Greta?" Wings' face was pure confusion. "Your old maid?"

"Dutch," I said, looking him straight in the face, "did you kill Tango McColl?"

Dutch bit his lip again.

Wings shook the man even harder. "You better answer her, man."

Dutch whimpered. "I only wanted to be a part of it. I've always wanted to be a part of it. You guys are so cool."

Dee shook his head. His voice cracked in disbelief. "Why would you kill Tango?"

Dutch swallowed. "I didn't want to. H-he made me."

"Made you?" Wings snarled. "You little—"

I placed a hand on Wings' shoulder to stop him, then turned back to Dutch. "What do you mean he made you?"

Dutch's eyes shot to Hips, who took a reflexive step back under the roadie's gaze. "I told him about Hips."

"The arthritis?" I asked.

Dutch nodded.

"Arthritis?" Dee repeated.

I waved him off, continuing with Dutch. "And what did Tango do?"

"He… He laughed at me." Dutch's voice grew angry, sputtering between whimpers and rage. "He said Hips would be a better guitar player than me even if he had no fingers at all."

"And that made you angry."

Dutch's eyes were red and bulgy. "I gave everything to this band! Everything. You guys had it all. Took it all. If Hips had to leave, that opened a spot for me. But Tango said no." Dutch licked his lips faster now. "He promised me a spot for years then said no!" Dutch squirmed wildly under Dee and Wings' restraints, but they held him firm. Dutch breathed heavily for a moment, then continued, "If Tango wasn't going to give me my spot, then I was going to take it. It's what I deserved. Tango deserved everything he got, just like me!"

I exhaled slowly to keep calm. "And what about Hips? That was for Greta, wasn't it?"

Dutch's eyes once again cast toward the crowd. His voice was weak. "If I were lead singer..."

"Lead singer?" Wings roared. The guitarist stood, still grasped harshly onto Dutch's shoulder and straddled

the man, then drew back an arm and punched Dutch so
hard the roadie blacked out once again.

Nineteen

"No, Miss Lewis, you cannot say just one more thing," Deputy Todd growled. "You've said quite enough already. It seems every time you call there's yet another unconscious man you claim is a murderer. This is what, two just today?"

"But I've been trying to tell you he's—"

"Ah!" Deputy Todd held up a firm hand.

I turned away with a scowl. Ryan, Angie and Harper, who waited nearby, rushed over. Mayor Dewey flopped in Harper's arms.

"What did he say?" Angie asked. "Is he going to arrest him?"

I shrugged. "He wouldn't even let me finish."

"Incompetent fool," Harper hissed. "Thinks he's got everything under control until it bops him on the head."

Ryan placed an arm around my shoulder. "Are you okay?"

I nodded. "Just shaken." Then I realized he was still in his full Highland get-up. "You look great. I'm so sorry

I missed your bagpipes."

He squeezed me close. "Aye, I'll play them again later. Besides, Ethan wasn't nearly as mortified as I'd hoped."

"Where is Ethan now?" I looked around, trying to spot him over the crowd. Most people still lingered, gossiping like chickens after the excitement of Dutch's slip and slide across the stage and subsequent confession.

Ryan pointed toward the kennels. "He's with Daisy. Seemed to take a liking to her."

Angie squealed. "Oh, Ryan, please tell me you're taking her home?"

"Aye," he said with a chuckle. "The newest member of clan MacKenzie."

I leaned into Ryan's hug. "That's a great idea. A dog will be perfect for him."

Harper nodded toward the stage. "Looks like ol' Flabbypants is finally waking up."

Dutch had risen enough to sit up and held his head in his hands. The other band members stood to the side, Slomo with a giant paw on Wings' chest to hold him back from attacking Dutch again. Dee and Hips looked dazed.

At the sight of me, Dutch recoiled and tried to scramble to his feet, but the oil still coated his shoes and he fell onto his backside.

Deputy Todd placed a firm hand on the roadie's shoulder. "Stay right there, Dutch, or whatever your real name is."

I was thankful Deputy Todd didn't simply disregard my accusation and the first-hand accounts of Dutch's confession and let the man go. But this was the best opportunity for him to assert his authority, and I was sure he couldn't pass up the moment.

"You're under arrest, Dutch…" Deputy Todd looked around irritably. "Would someone tell me what the heck this man's real name is?"

Finally, Hips stepped forward. His eyes were sad, a mix of grief and betrayal. "His name is Dennis Janssen, and I thought he was my friend."

***

"I can't believe it was Dutch all along." Angie hunkered deeply in one of my library's club chairs and took a wide-eyed sip from her coffee mug. "He seemed so nice."

Harper snorted, startling Mayor Dewey who slept in her lap like a furry orange log. "His crush on Greta should've been the first red flag."

Angie's light brown curls shook gently. "I guess love makes us do strange things. Are you going to keep his tambourine?"

Greta gave the instrument a shake, and the clang of the chimes filled the library. "Wouldn't be my first gift from a felonious suitor."

"Gosh," Angie said, "I don't know how I'd feel if I found out I was the reason a man was almost murdered."

Harper's hands flew up. "Let's not give the old bag too much credit. Dutch was clearly on a dark path to begin with."

I considered Greta, with her long, stringy gray hair and drabby garb. "I guess his infatuation with Greta was the final straw. You all heard what he admitted on that stage after he was arrested. He'd been trying to get a spot in that band for decades, and Tango strung him along. With the singer out of the way, Dutch knew he could squeeze in."

"Yeah," Harper said, "and I'm supposed to believe that he was willing to kill that Hips guy next just to impress *Greta*?"

I shrugged. "He said he thought being the lead singer would be his ticket into her affections."

"You're a regular *femme fatale*, Greta." Angie giggled then caught herself and covered her mouth with a hand, looking abashed.

Greta grunted. "Meh."

Harper turned a keen eye toward the old woman. "You're awfully quiet about all this."

She tapped the tambourine's drum. Thump, thump. "Have other things on my mind."

"Like what?" I asked.

Thump. "Like that church wall."

"Oh, right." Angie sat up straighter in the club chair. "I'd almost forgotten with all the pageant festivities and, you know, murders."

"And what are we supposed to do about it?" Harper peered around at each of us in turn. "We can't just waltz into the church and say, 'Oh, hi there, Pastor Basil. Any hidden pirate treasure about? No? Well, don't mind us while we snoop around a bit, maybe pull up a few flagstones or tear down a wall or two.'"

I couldn't help but agree. The X may have marked the spot on the church wall, but our next steps were unclear. *Do we need next steps?* "What if we stop?" I asked.

Harper's face scrunched. "Stop what?"

"Stop looking. Stop searching. Just let it be?"

Angie's voice was weak, almost wounded. "If that's what you want, Poppy."

"What?" Harper swiveled and shot Angie a scathing glare before turning to me. "We are absolutely *not* giving up on this. In the past year, I have been kidnapped, shot at, and almost buried alive with a musty, dusty gold-toothed skeleton, so I am not going to let us just walk away from this."

Greta thumped the tambourine lightly. "The cat lady's right."

Harper did a double-take.

Greta continued, "We can't give up because we aren't the only ones looking. And if it's not us, it will be the Gold Hand."

"What then?" I asked. "We've been chasing this supposed treasure forever. What's so horrible if Everett Goodwin gets ahold of it?"

Harper rose to her feet, fuming. Dewey oozed from her lap and curled up in her vacated cushion. "His henchmen shot at us, Poppy. If this is your story, then he's the evil villain. Don't forget he stayed in your house pretending to be someone else. How creepy is that? This dude is not a good person."

"All right," I said. "Sit down, please. I guess I'm tired from all the running around."

Harper scooped up Dewey and plopped back into the chair.

"You deserve a break," Angie said to me. "And I suggest we all go to bed and get some rest. We aren't thinking straight when we're exhausted."

Rolling her eyes, Harper said, "It's only six in the evening, Angie."

The pudgy woman's eyes shot to the clock on the wall. "Oh, my. Well, I get up earlier than the rest of you."

"We should sleep on it though," I said. "There's not much we can do until the Gold Hand makes a move. In the meantime, I have a house full of moping musicians who are processing a lot. Don't forget, they lost their band manager, too."

"What will they do?" Angie asked.

"I heard Cherry's going to manage the band. They'll need to find another member now that Dutch is gone."

Greta rattled her tambourine.

"Not you," I said quickly. "Why don't you get some tea going for our guests instead?"

As Greta ambled through the door of the library, I turned to my friends. "I'm sorry I gave up there for a moment. With Tango's murder and Greta's arrest, not to mention Lily outstaying her welcome, I've had a lot on my plate."

Angie rubbed my arm. "It's okay. We understand."

"It's time for me to head out, anyway," Harper said. She tucked Dewey under an arm and rose from her chair.

"Where are you going?" I asked.

"I, uh, have plans."

"Plans?" My eyebrow rose.

She shuffled toward the door, avoiding eye contact. "It's nothing. Just a quick dinner."

Angie's face lit up. "Dinner?"

Harper huffed and tucked a loose curl behind her headband. "Now don't make a big deal, okay. I'm meeting Charlie for dinner."

"Charlie!" Angie clapped her hands, clearly delighted at the idea. "A date!"

"It's not a date," Harper shot back. "Just dinner."

"You gave me plenty of grief when I used to say my

dinners with Ryan weren't dates."

"Yeah, but…" Harper squirmed and shifted Dewey to her other arm. "It's just dinner."

Angie continued to clap, adding a few twirls and hops of excitement. "Can I cater your wedding?"

Harper's eyes rolled dramatically as she reached for the library door handle.

"Aren't you forgetting something?" I couldn't hide the twinge of a smile that touched the corner of my mouth.

Harper looked at me curiously.

I nodded toward a side table.

"Oh, yeah." Hoisting Mayor Dewey over a shoulder, Harper scooped up the gleaming three-tiered trophy with both hands. "Can't forget this. I'll drop it in Town Hall when I clean out Mista Vista's cat box.

The End of Book 5

Lucinda Harrison is a writer and crafter who lives in northern California with her two mischievous cats. She is the author of the Poppy Lewis Mystery series.

Connect online at lucindaharrisonauthor.com

BOOKS BY LUCINDA HARRISON

Poppy Lewis Mystery Series
Murder in Starry Cove
Best Slayed Plans
A Foul Play
Dead Relatives
Shock & Roll